'What a bracing, [...] the ability of nat[ure...] *Undertow* is a gripp[ing...] world and the human spirit. It made me want to live more, seek adventure, find an albatross.'
—Meg Bignell

# UNDERTOW
## KIM BAMBROOK

© Kim Bambrook 2022
kimbambrook.com

ISBN: 978-0-6455101-0-2

All rights reserved.
No part of this publication may be reproduced,
stored in a retrieval system, or transmitted,
in any form or by any means either electronic,
mechanical, by photocopying, recording or otherwise,
without prior permission of the author.

Cover photograph by Doug Thost
dougthostphotography.zenfolio.com

Author photograph by Karen Wilson-Megahan
kwilsonphotography.com

Published by Forty South Publishing Pty Ltd
Hobart, Tasmania
fortysouth.com.au

Printed by McPherson's Printing Group
Melbourne, Victoria
mcphersonsprinting.com.au

For my mother, Irene,
who took my hand on slow walks
as we listened to the birds,
and who never stopped believing in me,

and to my father, Graeme,
a big presence,
a bushman,
a raconteur,
and a family man.

one
# Missing

I roll onto my back and drag the pillow across my face. Sunlight bursts through the hatch and floods my bed. I'm not ready to wake up. Water slides under the hull, gently propelling *Mulwala* through the water. *I wonder why we are not anchored up in Cloudy Bay yet?* That had been the plan before I took to bed with a killer headache.

'Sam,' I call.

No answer.

Sighing, I hoist myself into a sitting position and rub sleep from my eyes. Rolls of navigation maps, hanging in netting above my head, sashay from side to side like lazy swimmers.

'I'm awake,' I call out loudly, hoping Sam will hear me above the steady throbbing of the engine.

I wriggle out of the cabin and grab a mug out of the sink. Downing a glass of water, I shake my drug-fuzzed head clear.

*Damn migraine medication.*

The main cabin takes on a grey hue. A glance out the window tells me that fog is encroaching upon *Mulwala*. I call out to Sam as I haul myself up the companionway steps.

'Morning,' I say, smile at the ready.

Sam is not at the helm. I stick my head back inside the cabin in case I've missed seeing him down there. Perhaps he's in the forward cabin where we store our boating paraphernalia.

'Sam,' I yell.

No answer.

I look around the vessel in confusion, taking in the fluttering of the headsail, the steady rise and fall of the bow and the straight line of the mast. There is no sign of Sam on the boat.

Turning to the stern, I step onto the aft deck and peer into the water as it washes away from *Mulwala*'s sleek lines. The wake disappears into the fog. The dinghy is safely raised on davits above the stern, and below it, securely attached to the boat railing, is the lifebuoy.

I cup my hands around my mouth. 'Where are you, Sam?' I scream, my voice flat across the water.

Staring at the rotating wheel of the helm, I can't believe Sam is not standing there with a cheery good morning, and an explanation as to why *Mulwala* is not at anchor.

My mind is spinning as I look beyond the vessel, seeking a reassuring glimpse of Sam's red life jacket.

Frantic now, I scream until my lungs hurt, straining to see beyond the fog to where land ought to have been. There is only the sea, rolling and endless.

two
# Red

The creak of the wheel as it makes slight adjustments is unnerving. I steady myself as my eyes search the yacht. In vain I hope that Sam will materialise. My heart is beating hard against the wall of my chest as I thrust the throttle back to idle. I scurry along the decking towards the bow of *Mulwala,* crouching low as I push aside the headsail – slack in the still air. I lean as far as I dare over the railing. Failing to see more than a few metres ahead of the bow, I curse the dense fog.

'Sam, answer me!' I shout.

Still no answer bar the screech of a lone gull as it dips towards me, seemingly affronted by all the noise I'm making.

*Mulwala* is on autopilot, and I feel as if I am too, so surreal is this situation. Cursing, I do another sweep of the boat looking for clues. Nothing is out of place. There is no sign of Sam, no sign of a life jacket, nothing but water and this crazy fog.

My greatest sailing fear, to be alone at sea, no land in sight, has been realised. Sam is not on the boat. And, as improbable as it is, this is my reality. Anger wells up within me.

*Damn you, Sam, you can't just disappear; not now you have made a sailor out of this landlubber.*

Water shifts under the yacht. I lift my hand above the navigation console. My finger hovers for the briefest of moments before I press the Man Overboard button, marking a GPS waypoint at my current location. I never wanted to press this button.

It signals a search for a missing person.

It signals that I am now alone.

I'm finding it hard to breathe. I have no idea what has happened to Sam, nor *where* he is now.

*How long can someone survive in the Southern Ocean at the tail end of summer?*

Visibility is poor and I can't even see land, let alone anything else.

The screen on the chart plotter is set at close range. I zoom out, seeking an identifiable landform on the map in front of me. We're a long way off course, well south of our intended destination, Bruny Island. A tremor runs through me. The last thing I recall is leaving Partridge Island under motor, with clear skies and barely a breath of wind; a bit of breeze is needed to set sails. At some stage the wind must have picked up enough for Sam to put the headsail up. When it died out, fog had crept in.

The sail slaps and stirs me into action. I quickly furl it and resume my position at the wheel. My brow furrows as I realise that Sam most likely went overboard while there was still puff in the sail. No way would Sam leave it flapping about like that.

The sea swell looks to be around two metres and building, as it is usually does ahead of a southerly front. The map shows that I am around five nautical miles south of Pedra Branca, the island itself approximately twenty-six nautical miles south of the most southerly point of mainland Tasmania. That we are so far off course is as perplexing as Sam's disappearance.

I fill my lungs then exhale loudly, trying to calm my nerves as I prepare to turn *Mulwala* back in the direction we've come from, navigating from the MOB point on the chart plotter. I switch from autopilot back to manual steering and plant my legs apart, toes gripped for purchase. Directing the bow of the boat to the north, I want to retrace our passage. I wait for the next wave, then push the throttle forward and turn the wheel.

*Mulwala* responds as she is built to do, rolling with the sea, throwing water aside and obeying my command to turn.

---

A glance at the compass – resting in its clear bulbous housing directly behind the navigation console – assures me of our direction and verifies the position reading marked on the instrumentation panel. Confounded, I turn the helm a few degrees eastwards, back towards Bruny.

I usually love this feeling, surfing down the face of a wave with the sea at our stern, swell pushing *Mulwala* forward. Swift passage gives me a momentary burst of courage.

'Where are you?' I call, my voice blaring in the eerie fog.

A menacing atmosphere pervades. The sea banks and falls, hiding whatever is in its keeping. I have no idea how much time has elapsed since I retreated to my bunk as we left pretty Partridge Island. Somehow, I have lost track of time, lost Sam, lost my holiday high, and I am lost at sea.

Reaching for the handset, I note the GPS coordinates as they were when I had pressed the MOB and get ready to make a mayday call. Planes deployed to search in a grid area would have more chance than I would of spotting a red lifejacket. The Southern Ocean is not kind to those who linger too long in her chilly embrace. Suddenly, *Mulwala* is jolted by a rogue wave smacking us on the beam. I activate the radio.

'Mayday, mayday, mayday, this is *Mulwala, Mulwala, Mulwala*, does anyone copy me?'

I repeat my entreaties for help and for my efforts get nothing but radio silence. Only then do I look down at the instrument panel. It's blank.

The twelve-volt house battery switch might have taken a knock. The boat's electronic navigational system needs battery power or it doesn't work. If you ask me, it's in a stupid position, that battery panel; it's so easily jolted. The electronics had been on before I tried to make the mayday call. I silently pray the answer is as simple as turning a switch back to the on position.

Gazelda – our wind generator – starts to hum. A puff of wind blows against my cheek. I look up and see that a light breeze has started to shift the fog. To keep the helm straight while I am below deck, I lock the wheel in place with bungee cords.

With *Mulwala*'s helm now fixed to ensure the swell is behind us, I fight the urge to rush. *Survival depends on keeping calm.* Easier said than done. I'm not even close to being calm.

*What if I miss seeing Sam while I'm below deck?*

I vault down the companionway steps, grasping the grab rails for purchase. Checking the battery panel, I see that its switch is in the correct position. *Then the fault must be with the instrumentation.* I glance up at the control panel above the navigation station and immediately see that, even though the switches are in the correct position, no lights are on. Diving across the cabin I reach for the Phillips head screwdriver, conveniently located at the front of the navigation table. With legs braced as *Mulwala* pitches, I flip the panel of the fuse board forward, checking for a blown fuse.

Instantly, I see a main power feed to the fuse board – a red wire – has corroded and is not attached to the terminal. Without that red wire, no thicker than my little finger, I have no instrumentation and no radio. It hits me hard. I have no power and no idea if I can restore it. As a scream rises from deep in my gut, *Mulwala* bucks and my legs are kicked from under me.

three
# Pedra Branca

I'm flung unceremoniously across the cabin, floundering, as *Mulwala* surfs down a wave. Crashing onto the floor, I narrowly avoid hitting my head on the side of the galley bench as the boat dips and is pushed broadside to the sea. The air is punched out of me. Wrapping my arms around my chest, I roll into a ball and stay that way until I catch my breath.

*Mulwala* rocks and rolls as she rights herself. I hoist myself up and fumble my way to the companionway steps. When I'm back on deck, there is no mistaking what I see. Ahead and to port there's a monstrous rock, the size of an eighteen-story building, which has materialised above the churning water – and *Mulwala* is being swept towards it. This is a rock I know well from many pictures and stories. Pedra Branca, punching skywards, has emerged from behind a foggy veil to tower threateningly above the sea.

Reflexively, I dive for the wheel and see that the bungee cords are no longer secure. I thrust them on deck, kick them aside and turn the wheel to starboard, away from Pedra. The vessel has taken a nasty knock and I can feel her shuddering as I pull the helm around.

While I was below deck, a southerly front had hit with sudden and dangerous force. The wind has picked up alarmingly and the ocean is hungry. As the yacht slides into a trough, the craggy island in front of us is hidden from view. I hold my position and keep the bow pointed away from Pedra. Everything I have learnt in my years of sailing comes to the fore as I work with the boat to get us out of danger. The strong easterly current is not helping my cause, meeting the opposing wind and creating steep fronted waves. The opposing forces of wind and sea are sucking *Mulwala* towards Pedra, dragging her close to perilous shores.

The conditions are more challenging than I have ever seen. Fishermen and sailors speak with respect of this notorious region and I am seeing firsthand why. I'm sweating like crazy and I know it's due to terror.

Pedra Branca disappears from sight regularly as we ride the rolling sea. Checking the yacht's position, I grasp at the unlikely scenario that we can creep away from reef and rocks. When we are in open water I can heave-to with our sea anchor and try to regain use of our instrumentation – surely, there must be a way – and radio for help.

The fog has been replaced by dark, low-lying clouds, and the waves chopping and frothing. I no longer have the aid of the depth sounder on our chart plotter. While I can make out Eddystone and Sidmouth rocks to the east – both prominent – there is a lot under the water that I cannot see. Without electronic navigation, my life is in my hands alone. And so, I think, is Sam's.

Sam is my constant boating companion. And I am his. I have never skippered a vessel on my own before today, but I do have years of sailing experience. I have sailed with Sam, and years prior with a crazy but skilled skipper on a different sea, far away. I survived a storm then and will do so again. If I maintain a visual and keep control of the helm, I can navigate us to safety. Sailors of old had neither depth sounders nor radios but they found a way, as will I.

*What choice do I have?*

I hang on, guiding *Mulwala* in increments, striving to gain ground and get clear of rock. The current rushes and sucks at our hull, making headway more and more difficult. I feel the helm lurch and shudder under my hands.

The wind is intensifying and becoming increasingly loud. Waves are crashing like cymbals, the spray drenching me. Despite my efforts, *Mulwala* is being directed more by the sea than me. As if in a boxing ring, I know I am making the right moves but still my opponent batters me mercilessly.

Lightning punctures the sky to the west. The worst of the front is yet to hit.

As I struggle to hold *Mulwala* steady, I push the throttle further forward, trying desperately to gain ground. The boat groans. Come on, *Mulwala*! Suddenly the wheel is violently wrenched from under my hands. It swings of its own accord, thrashing side to side, as if daring me to go near. Not able to hold it, the helm takes on a life of its own. If I reach for it, I could lose an arm.

Helplessness washes over me as heavy as the sea. Time slows as I cling onto the centre console. Collapsing onto the deck, I hold on. Looking up, I see grey walls of water that build and topple, like buildings in a giant Lego land.

*Is this the final scene?*

As if from above, I look down on this tiny figure clinging to a drowning vessel. There's a voice in my head, urging me to hold on, telling me to get up. It's Matt, it's my son. His faith in me has never wavered, despite times of uncertainty. Resolve germinates. I will escape this torment, as I did that ocean rip when I was a young teenager, and my first fear-filled sailing adventure almost as long ago. I will find Sam. I will make it home to my family. I shake my head, clearing it, and wipe my arm across my eyes as I haul myself up.

four
# Baja: The testing ground

Sailing experiences were non-existent in my childhood. I was nineteen when I signed up to crew on a yacht departing from San Diego. It was then that I experienced my first great adventure, away from the protected confines of my childhood home. I met the greater world, such as it is, both wonderful and terrible. I swore then that I would never return to the sea. But I did return, many years later, and when I did there were many days I would ask myself, *why?*

I love the land, the feel of the earth. Growing up on a dairy farm amidst rolling hills in picturesque East Gippsland ensured that. There, I experienced the warm gooey sensation of fresh cow manure between my toes, jumping in puddles, and climbing trees. We celebrated when the dams were full and I learnt, from a young age, to respect water. I discovered how powerful it could be on a family holiday to Tathra in New South Wales. Along with my older sister, I got caught in a rip and was sucked out well beyond the breakers.

'Don't fight the current,' she called out. 'Stay calm and swim across it.'

She knew the ocean better than me. The weight, the huge hungry entity that was the ocean enticed for the same reasons that it instilled in me an acute wariness that was to stay with me thereafter. I was lured by the unknown, despite unseen perils.

## UNDERTOW

The farm was my playground. I could roam barefoot and carefree with my siblings, my companions. We explored the bush on the mountain behind our home, swam in dams, and built cubby houses under the tank stand and in the hayshed. Once I convinced two school friends to camp with me below the mountain for a weekend. Dad helped us haul our gear to my pre-chosen campsite, and then we were alone. I set up a tent for the first time. We hardly slept a wink that night as animals emerged from the bush and scared the bejesus out of us. I loved it just the same.

I left school and flew to the USA. My plan was to trek through national parks between Mexico and Alaska. I wanted to hike and was looking for mountains to climb. The excitement that I felt when I landed in Los Angeles was quickly dampened by the enormity of the challenge I had set myself. Coming from a small Australian country town, I had never seen such a busy place as the Los Angeles International Airport. I succumbed to self-doubt. *How will I survive?* I spent weeks acclimatising, hiking in forests where trees towered above me and looked and smelled nothing like the eucalypts of home.

I hitched a ride on the back of a motorbike to the start of a hiking trail in Southern California. When I got there, a message on a San Diego backpackers' noticeboard caught my eye. Harry, a skipper with decades of sailing under his belt, was looking for a crew. I was enticed by his salty tales of adventure. Harry owned a fifty-foot sloop: a single-masted sailing boat bound for the West Indies via the Baja California and the Panama Canal. Ocean adventures were not on my radar and I had no boating skills to speak of, but that didn't stop me. With youthful blind confidence and a zest for new experiences, I applied and was quickly hired as a crew member, cook, and first aid officer. My romantic ideals came to life as I embraced this new adventure.

On the eve of our departure, Harry took us, his eager crew of three, to the San Diego Yacht Club for a pre-sail celebration. My horizons were expanding. I was embracing new experiences. With adrenaline coursing through me, I went to bed that night knowing sleep would not come easily. My spirits were high as I lay staring into the darkness, wondering what the new day would bring.

We were headed to the West Indies where Harry had property. 'A woman is waiting for me there,' he said, with a broad grin and his chest puffed out.

My equally inexperienced crewmates were a sweet couple, teachers from a Sydney primary school. We looked to each other for reassurance. We were in this together.

I read what I could in the limited preparation time I had for the voyage. I was excited at the prospect of going through the Panama Canal. I imagined what it would be like to be aboard a vessel as it was spat out of the canal lock's embrace and into the Atlantic Ocean. Vague thoughts of pirates and big seas entered my mind. For the most part, I was filled with anticipation for the journey ahead.

I know now that the Pacific Ocean, off the west coast of the Baja Peninsula, is not for the faint-hearted. After setting sail from San Diego and crossing the Mexican border, Harry gave us an introduction to her wicked wiles by docking at Tijuana, our first port of call in Mexico. We stocked up on whisky and *Penthouse* magazines, supposedly for trade. Our captain then took his crew to a local bar. It smelt like a gutter and resembled a farm shed in its disarray.

'This will test ya backbones,' Harry laughed as he led us to the bar.

I turned on my barstool as an announcement was made. Rowdy applause from the other patrons, mostly sailors, followed, and a mule was positioned centre stage. A scantily-clad woman approached the animal. She offered up softly spoken words as she stroked the trembling creature. Her words obviously soothed and the mule was enticed into sexual stimulation by deft hands. Rousing cries from this rough bunch of seamen exploded in my eardrums. My innocence was shaken. I felt my childhood slipping away. Tears threatened. I left the bar and found comfort and familiarity in an icy pole bought from a young street vendor. I was still a kid, wanting to taste adulthood but still needing icy poles.

Recollections of that voyage are like snapshots that have been thrown into a pile in no particular order. It wasn't all bad. Baja California, away from the tourist haunts, was beautiful. My memories linger. I can summon the smell of tortillas being cooked on a rusty forty-four-gallon drum set in sand on the beach drifting across the water as we sailed past a tiny village. I would have given a lot for one of those tortillas.

I remember a dead whale, beached, vultures ripping flesh off its hulking body. That memory is painted red and black. I drag images of the sea forth but feel more than I see; huge, lonely walls of steel-grey water pushed up by the Pacific plates below as they rub together.

I was frightened as I scaled the mast to make repairs while the rest of the crew lay stricken with sea sickness. We sailed far out to sea, heading south in the unrelenting weather. After leaving Tijuana, we didn't see land again for two weeks. I wrote in my journal, both for comfort and to try and make sense of these new experiences. I wrote about my fearful body tremors, more apparent when sails were reefed because it was so difficult in big swells. Winds often heightened to gale force and I struggled to move safely around the vessel. The Pacific Ocean, endlessly flowing and undisturbed by any visible land mass for many days at a time, was the stuff of nightmares for years to come.

When we came to shelter in Magdalena Bay after turbulent weeks at sea, I finally slept. We were a good distance offshore – deemed safer than being close to land in gale-force winds and storms. Struggling as I was awoken from my deep sleep, I was reluctant but convinced to get back up on deck. I was met by an astounding sight. Pacific gray whales, all the way from the Bering Sea in Alaska, come to that particular lagoon to breed every spring. Intrigued by our boat, the whales erupted from the lagoon, sending waves of water washing over us. Barnacles – seemingly as big as dinner plates – encrusted areas of the whales' vast bodies, yet they sliced clean and pure from the water towards the sky, all grace and majesty. Our captain had sailed us safely into a charming bay in time to see a marvel of nature.

I jumped ship with my crewmates – all of us equally relieved – at Cabo San Lucas at the southernmost point of Baja. Harry shrugged as we left.

'This lot show a bit more promise than you three,' he said, after we introduced him to our hastily sought-after replacements. They were all far more experienced and worldly than we were.

'Thank you' was not a phrase in Harry's vocabulary. I shrugged my backpack on. I had no regrets. I had taken a chance and weathered some storms. Now I felt more connected to life than I ever had been. I finally understood why people pushed boundaries in their quests for adventure. I was hooked.

five
# Mulwala

*Mulwala*'s struggle has been impressive. Battling the East Australian Current and opposing south-westerly swell has forced her to her limits. But we are both now tiring as we fight for our survival.

I struggle to stand as the strengthening wind drowns my curses, increases in pitch and sucks us closer to mighty Pedra. Desperately, I manage to grab hold of the wheel as every muscle in my body is stretched taut and I fight to hold on to *Mulwala*. I'm thrown violently from side to side, the wheel dictating direction, not me. In its current state the helm is a useless tool, thrashing backwards and forwards like a gyrating dancer on a disco floor.

Whitewater breaks over the gunnels and drenches me. The wheel is ripped from my hands and I'm thrown onto the deck. Above the cry of the angry storm, I hear the harsh ripping of the headsail, which has unfurled and is being torn apart. I try to pull myself up but my timing is out. *Mulwala* cops the impact of a wave on the beam. Falling hard against the locker behind the throttle, I lunge forward from my waist to grip the end of the tether, which is attached to the lifeline in the centre of the cockpit. I had automatically attached the loose end of the tether to my harness when I came back on deck, and I'm momentarily relieved. I feel more security being in the middle of the deck, although I'm unsure if that's an illusion.

Clumsily, I push up onto my knees, my hair wrapping itself every which way around my face and slapping me sharply in the eyes. As if imploring, I thrust one arm forward towards the crazily spinning wheel as I edge my way to the helm. My resolve is great and I manage to secure the helm once more. It is but for a moment, my strength no match against the wheel, which wrenches of its own volition, as if possessed, and then abruptly stops. With a brutal kick, I'm thrown down. This time I don't get up. Either the steering cable has broken or I've lost the rudder. It doesn't matter which, for I know in that instant the storm has beaten us.

I crawl around the helm and reach for the middle cockpit locker. Despite the wind's resistance, I manage to open it and push aside ropes to reveal our emergency grab bag. Pulling it clear of the locker, I slide to a sitting position, secure the bag between my knees and hold on to it tightly. Fearing I'll faint – my breath as laboured as if I'd run a marathon – I suck air up from the bottom of my diaphragm and blow out as steadily as I can through pursed lips. My pulse starts to normalise and I roll onto the deck.

Curling into a fetal position, I fold myself around the precious bag of supplies. The incessant howling of the storm fades. My senses dull. I am indifferent as my body slides, jerking across the deck in time to the bucking of the vessel. I curl up into a tighter ball as my back hits the locker. Grieving that Sam is no longer at my side, I know that soon *Mulwala* will flounder and lose her battle, succumbing to the sea. Stories of Sam's and my sailing adventures are etched into the vessel's sleek lines, and these *Mulwala* will take with her.

A memory flashes across my mind. My father had built bookshelves for our boat; Sam had installed them. He had also fashioned a vase that could be secured to the mast below deck. As we celebrated our new home, Sam regularly brought me flowers, and I stocked the bookshelves. Our boat is a home of memories, shared meals, love, laughter, tears and joy, as every home should be.

Water falls in torrents from the sky, thrusts over the yacht's gunnels, bow and stern, and washes over my body like a waterfall. The boat is thrown about as readily as a cork in a bottle. There's a sharp jolt and a jagged, harrowing sound rises from inside me, escaping in a howl of pain and terror. Grasping the cockpit table, I force myself to stand, one arm holding securely onto the grab bag. The boat is taking a beating. Intractable rivers of dark water streams over our vessel's sides, pouring down the decking, picking up stray lines and anything not tied down. A sailing glove washes over my leg and is gone, off the stern in a blink. Looking down the companionway steps I see the galley is awash.

The headsail flaps frantically, torn to strips, a pretty sheet no more. As my eyes slide upwards towards the rising bow of *Mulwala*, she noses up towards the north-eastern corner of Pedra Branca, thrusts high, then falls away again effortlessly. Unbelievably, *Mulwala* is showing me a way, giving me a chance. The yacht has turned a full 180 degrees back towards the island and is now facing the lowest point of the land.

After momentary inertia, a flood of adrenaline fuels my body. Knowing I must get my timing right, knowing that this corner of Pedra Branca has a kelp bed to soften an approach, knowing that a rock ledge lies beyond a slippery ramp, I am being offered a chance to take a leap of faith. My heart hammers against my chest wall so hard I'm sure I can hear it. I have mere seconds to make this decision and will get one chance only. Relocating the tether to the portside lifeline, I pull myself forward on slippery, icy cold rails, hauling the tether with me. Once on the bow, I dare not look down, my movements dictated by the rise and fall of the boat. Hand on my harness's tether clip, I stand tall, poised to release myself from the yacht's death throes as her bow pierces the top of the next wave.

With barely a pause to look at what lies below, I detach myself from my umbilical cord to *Mulwala* and leap out as far as I can away from the yacht. On invisible wings, I am for the briefest of moments airborne, the yacht's hull rising above me before she is sucked back by the sea. As I fall into the tumbling water, the grab bag flies up from where I had positioned it – across my shoulder and low on my front – and hits me in the face. I taste blood. Darkness engulfs me as water closes over my head. I am briefly submerged, involuntarily sucking in water before the life jacket self-inflates, the pressure pushing me to the surface of the sea. Gasping, coughing, laughing, crying, I can scarcely believe I have survived.

Kelp slaps relentlessly against my body and instinctively I wrap the thick, rubbery branches several times around my arms, anchoring me. Years of diving with Sam has provided valuable lessons. The bull kelp licks at me, whipping backwards and forwards in the surge. Kelp cuddling, Sam called it, although it feels more like kelp wrestling in my current circumstances. Gasping between the onslaughts of waves, I fight to get air into my lungs. I'm flung to and fro with the kelp, loosening my hold as water pushes me towards rock, then tightening my grip once more as I am sucked back with the retreating sea, just as Sam had taught me to do.

The collar of my jacket rides up to my nose and helps me from swallowing more water. I sense *Mulwala*, a dark shadow drifting away from me on a receding wave. I wrench my head around to look but already she is diminishing in white wash. She will likely end up on the reef at the bottom of the sea, locked in a kelp forest's embrace, a new home for the sea life below.

I choke back a forlorn sob as I check my position in relation to the shore, kelp dancing and winding around me. My inflated life jacket, wet clothes, and compromising sea conditions are making conscious movements more difficult. I know not to fight the swell, to save energy and to trust the sea as she moves me as her own, despite the natural inclination to do the opposite. The kelp on my arms is firm and I am ready to free myself of it. I gauge the swell and wait for the next wave to pick me up as white water bursts forth and bubbles explode up my nose.

The wave comes quickly and I'm tossed like a discarded toy. In an instant of blind panic, I fight the wave before fixing my eyes on the rock ahead of me. Tumbling through the churning sea, I cough and splutter as I'm thrown into a forest of kelp. As I blindly haul myself forward, another rush of water lifts me up and throws me.

My body freed of kelp, I land on solid rock. Despite my wet, heavy clothing and lacerated knees, I crawl forward as quickly as I can. Twisting my head, I see another wave coming and clamber further up the rock before the sea can reclaim me. With hand over hand and feet finding a hold, I scramble higher.

My confidence grows as I pass clips attached to the solid surface under me. These have been drilled into rock to allow researchers to clip themselves onto Pedra's lower reaches and ascend safely. Hope gives me renewed strength. Long minutes later I haul myself onto a rock shelf well above the waterline, my exhaustion and relief in equal parts immense.

*I've made it!*

I fall back, arms and legs splayed across the ledge as I take in huge gulps of air.

There is no deeper gratitude than that which is felt when life is spared. I don't know I'm crying until I taste the tears. A coughing fit ensues, and I roll over to purge myself of sea water.

Blood tinges the watery mess beneath my hands and knees. My ordeal is far from over, but I have defied the odds and survived thus far. This, alone, is miraculous. At my most depleted, a seed of resolve is planted.

## six
# Surviving Pedra

I sit with my legs splayed out in front of me and my back against firm rock. Immense relief surges through my body but I'm trembling with fatigue after the battering and my breath is ragged. From my vantage point, the wild sea below looks frightening. I shake my head looking at it, astounded to have made it to safe ground. I have scrambled up Pedra Branca's welcome ramp and am now around a third of the way up the north-eastern tip of the island.

I recall reading about Pedra with Sam before a sailing trip to Port Davey along Tasmania's South Coast. Researchers come here and camp on the island to study the prolific birdlife and a skink endemic to Pedra. The difference is that while researchers come here in calm conditions and of free will, I have escaped a sinking vessel, somehow managing to scramble ashore in one piece. Like the threatened skink, I too have defied the odds and survived.

Looking up I see inky black clouds, heavily weighted as they prepare to release their fill. One drop, two. Rain starts to fall in bullet-like bursts. A tumultuous clap of thunder reverberates through the rock below me. My grab bag is still slung snugly over my shoulder. My hip is aching, body battered and bruised, and my face is swollen from the punch of the bag where it had swung up and smacked me.

I hold my hands out in front of me. They are bloody and raw. The sight of the blood, red against the white splattered surface of the rock, pushes me to my feet as the rain starts to fall in earnest. Hastily now, with lightening scissoring the sky above me and wind cutting through my wet clothing, I retreat to the widest area of the ledge and press myself against the cold face of Pedra. Sliding down to sit, I draw my knees up and hug my bag, shivering convulsively.

I'm becoming numb and my fingers hurt as I flex them awkwardly. Logic finds a voice. I have to move fast and find the thermal blanket in the grab bag before hypothermia sets in. As I open the bag, my eyes fixate on the glaring high-vis safety sheet, a visible marker for rescue searchers. Pushing it under me, I scrounge through the bag until I find the lightweight thermal blanket, then rip open the covering with my teeth. I'm scared it will blow away. I hope for protection from the rain and cold rock. I'm protected from the worst of the westerly wind on this leeward side of the island and the shelf wall is a natural barrier. I wrap the thermal blanket around myself tightly, I try to hide from the elements.

Rain is seeping under my collar and forming a rivulet down my spine. I tuck myself into my makeshift shelter as securely as I can. I'm cocooned, thick plastic firm under me and the blanket pulled in close. I huddle beside the rock. I'm braver as I peep out at my surroundings.

I think of descriptions of the island that I have read. I'm fairly sure that my current location is where scientists set up tents when doing their work on the island. The flattish rock shelf appears well protected from the waves and sea spray that washes up onto Pedra's flank. It is east facing and so is ensured of some shelter from the southerly and westerly weather patterns predominant in these waters. I'm cautiously confident that I'm on the safest place on the rock for now. To move elsewhere is too hard to contemplate.

The emergency bag reminds me of a lucky dip. Reaching in carefully with one hand still firmly holding the sheet, I pull out a muesli bar. I don't hesitate as I tear open the packaging. Struggling not to eat the entire bar in a single gulp, I force myself to chew methodically. Not allowing for doubt that I will be rescued, I nonetheless have to conserve my resources. I'm going to have to prepare for a wait, and am already dreading how hard that will be.

My stomach growls loudly. I reach for the water bottle and swallow several mouthfuls. Before I eat or drink more, I secure the grab bag and set it between my knees. It is a relief to simply sit on the ground, my improvised shelter protecting me somewhat from the elements.

*That's better, Kay. Think of the positives. Use your head.*

I close my eyes, lean my head back and imagine sipping hot tea in a warm bath. It's a soothing thought and my body softens a little in response.

My eyelids are heavy despite the intense rain, regardless of the shrieking wind and the icy claws pulling at my shelter, probing and insistent. Shuffling back a little more, I curl into myself as tightly as I can and press up against the face of mighty Pedra. I count, one-cat-and-dog, two-cat-and-dog, anything to block out the horrible reality that I am in. I think of Sam spooning me under our doona and how easily I fall asleep when he does. I imagine being pulled into him as his body cushions my back, his arms enfolding me from behind.

I have slipped down into a lying position and realise I must have fallen asleep. Hauling myself up, my cheek pitted with pebble marks from resting on the rock floor, I lean against the wall. It's dark, and the sounds of the storm have intensified.

Rain on plastic creates a pinging sound and a staccato beat. Heavy rain has a bite to it. Being pounded upon, I am at the mercy of the elements and have no choice but to accept the storm's fury, loud and insistent. Pulling the blanket over my head, the only parts of me not covered are my nose and mouth. Amazed that the need to sleep is overwhelming in such harsh conditions, I fight the urge to succumb to fatigue once more, afraid that I won't wake up.

Against the raging storm, I can make out the sound of waves smashing against rock: a tremendous whacking noise. The sea must be huge as it races towards Pedra. It sounds like a freight train travelling at break-neck speeds to meet a scheduled drop-off. The noise is frightening; I picture the white water below, sea spray fuming upwards and towards me. It is a nightmare I want to end.

My lonely island, seemingly devoid of life in storms, is pummelled by the Southern Ocean. I imagine the little skinks scurrying into cracks and crevices when the weather turns wild. Pedra has a huge seal colony, and it is somehow comforting to imagine them deep in the sea around the island, insulated, blubber and fur keeping them warm. Burrowing deeper into my blanket, I shiver despondently, feeling lonelier than ever before.

I drift in and out of sleep. When next I form a conscious thought, I am aware of an absence. There are no cracks of thunder, no snaps of lightening. The rain has a steadier beat to it and the wind has ceased to howl intolerably; no longer is it trying to pull my blanket from me. I've wet my pants and I don't even have the strength to care.

Attempting to wriggle unresponsive toes, I reach down and knead my feet back to life. I massage my sore fingers, then curl them towards my mouth, blowing warm air into cupped hands. Moving a little, I rock first one way and then the other, stretching to get more comfortable and to encourage my blood to flow. Exhausted from these little actions, I drop my chin to my chest once more.

When next I open my eyes and dare to lift my head, I feel the cool kiss of night. Darkness hangs low and a shiver of wind disturbs the vast starless blanket of sky. A shadowed moon casts a dull light. Silhouetted against the rock, there stands beside me an albatross, curious and unafraid. I move, as if in a dream, and sense movement in turn. On graceful wings, the albatross rises lugubriously upwards, higher and higher, before being engulfed by the night sky. Laying my head atop the grab bag, I finally welcome sleep's embrace.

I dream of an albatross looking over me. How much time passes, I don't know; only that on waking, I am astounded to see that a new day is dawning.

seven

# Yosemite

The allure of beauty can be fraught with danger. Seeing photos of Yosemite while flicking through a *National Geographic* had helped to inspire my trip to the United States. Being young and travelling internationally for the first time, I had set my heart on hiking in beautiful places. I had tunnel vision. How I got to those places was irrelevant, as long as I could get there within my slender budget. Hiking in the Sierra Nevada Mountain range came before jumping on a sailboat and discovering how unpredictable the elements, and people, can be. I was enjoying hitchhiking and meeting new people. Thumbing a lift saved precious dollars.

I was still a teenager, yet well-practised in the art of hailing down passing traffic. The trick was to look confident and smile. Up to that point, my hitchhiking in California had proved to be uneventful. Without trepidation I thumbed a lift to Yosemite. After a circuitous route, a sightseeing tour free of charge – so the fellow who gave me a lift claimed (his nervous ticks making me nervous in turn) – I arrived safely at my destination. Perhaps it would have been wise to see that lift as a forewarning of the dangers to come.

Darkness had pulled the shades down over the valley long before my arrival. Wearily, I set up my tent. It would be daylight before I could take in the scenery of the national park. Early the next morning, as was my habit, I breakfasted on muesli and tea. The sky was starting to lighten and the campground was yet to stir as I wandered to a vantage point with my mug of tea in hand.

I nearly dropped my mug. It was *beautiful*. So picture-perfect that it almost hurt to look at it. I was quick to pull on my hiking boots. Sugar pines, heavy with snow, shook in the gentle early morning breeze and rained into already full creeks. Water gushed down streams, poured with unconstrained force over rocky falls and dazzled with reflective brilliance off snow-covered rocks and peaks. *Fairyland,* I imagined. I hiked up the appropriately named Mist Trail and was rewarded with glorious views. From the top of Vernal Falls, I gazed in rapt wonder as rainbows danced in the spray.

I literally skipped as I descended from the falls and could well have slid on the slippery trail if not for my trusty steel-toed hiking boots. Good grip was needed on the slick trail. I walked back to the campground at a slower pace, marvelling at the sparkling pools of ice melt as I went. The following day's hiking would be more ambitious; I would tackle a series of switchbacks to reach the higher Nevada Falls and beyond that, my ultimate goal, Half Dome.

Heading to happy hour at the Lodge Bar, I knew I would meet similarly cash-strapped backpackers. Fortifying myself with one glass of brandy and some popcorn, I saved my dollars and kept a clear head. I chatted to fellow hikers and backpackers – who didn't share my concerns for a clear head – and we discussed our plans for the following day. No one else had Half Dome on their agenda. Snowfalls had been heavy and in such conditions most hikers favoured lower altitude walks. Undeterred, I vowed to hike as far as I could up the enthralling rock formation. The forecast was for a clear day ahead.

With limited time and resources, I wanted to see as much as I could while in the park. Half Dome was a major drawcard. It loomed over the valley floor with grandeur, a mighty chunk of rotund granite with one side a vertical drop-off. It looked as if a giant knife had sliced through the dome with one clean cut. This was my opportunity to explore. I did not foresee danger; I saw opportunity.

Half Dome, with snow sliding off her cap over a rounded summit while her face captured sunlight trapped in icy crevices, was breathtaking. So much in the USA seemed magnified to me on that first trip, including trees, mountains and rocks. While Australia is a vast, dry and flat continent, everything seemed bigger and busier on that northern continent. Many years later I was to walk to Frenchmans Cap in Southwest Tasmania. It reminded me of Half Dome, but half the height of that mighty Yosemite monolith.

Words failed me when I arrived at the base of Half Dome. At over twice the size of the 700-metre-high Yosemite Falls – which had so impressed me the day before – it was the most imposing natural feature I had ever seen at close range. I realised then that I had underestimated the adventure. I didn't make it to the summit but had reward enough.

The occasional thud of snow falling from too heavy a branch above highlighted my sense of solitude. Sweat dripped as I ploughed through fresh snow. It was waist-deep in sections. A lone bear let me know of his presence but kept his distance. It was demanding. Exhausting. I had never hiked so hard and finally my heart sang as I descended to the valley floor below.

It had been a good day and, as it was raining and I was tired, I tucked myself into my sleeping bag early, book in hand, snug and warm. I had settled in comfortably when an inebriated backpacker demanded entry to my tent. I recognised him. He was, perhaps, a few years older than I, and had made previous advances towards me in the campground. He'd been at the bar earlier, drunk even then. I told him to leave but he wouldn't budge. Unzipping the tent, he half fell into my enclosure, the smell of alcohol strong on his breath.

Thinking quickly, I grabbed the bota bag – a leather wineskin that had been given to me as a gift before the hike. He wasn't going away, so I quickly thrust the bag towards him as a delay strategy, giving myself time to think. He smiled and took a swig of wine before handing it back to me. Red wine ran down his unkempt beard, his smirk revealing stained teeth and clear intentions. I pretended to drink with him, diverting him with small talk while we handed the wine back and forth between us. My mind was churning, heart racing.

When the wine was consumed, he lunged at me. My hastily formulated plan was put to the test. He was clumsy in his movements, as he loomed awkwardly over me in the small space of the tent. Wet lips pushed against my face. I made my move.

I always slept with my hiking boots, cushioned by clothing, under my head as a pillow. I grabbed them and, with all the force I could muster from my horizontal position, smashed the steel toes of the boots into his face. Aiming for his nose, I whacked him repeatedly, using every ounce of strength I had. Blood spurted immediately as he howled and fell aside. I hit out relentlessly. I continued with the blows, aiming for his nose, his face, scrambling to get loose from the confines of my sleeping bag while maintaining my attack.

Bloody faced, my assailant tried to deflect the thwack of the boots but was unsteady, and in the confined space he was the one now trapped.

'Stop! You're crazy,' he yelled above the noise of the rain, which was hammering down.

'Get out, get out,' I screamed in turn, assailing him with both boots and shrieks.

He struggled with the tent's zip as I maintained momentum, belting his head with all I had and consistently aiming for his nose as he dropped his arms to undo the zip. He fell through the fly-net entrance and still I hit out at him, falling myself partway through the tent entrance. The tent collapsed and I hit and pushed him until he tumbled from the nylon enclosure and fled into the black, wet night. Terrified he would come back, I quickly pulled on my pants, hesitating only to pick up my boots and coat, and I ran.

I will remember forever the beauty of Yosemite. The valley is truly a gift from nature, created with an artist's touch. My maturation was accelerated on that first trip abroad, lessons learned in Mexico and in Yosemite providing me with steep learning curves.

Nature is the best of teachers, the best of healers, and is my God. I would learn to work with her and to respect her power, generosity, and her many moods. Humankind, I decided, was far more dangerous. That night in Yosemite, the rain worked in my favour. As I hid in the toilet block until dawn, shivering with cold and delayed shock, the rain kept belting down and the man with the broken nose – for this damage I was sure I had inflicted – did not find me. I hitched out of the park at first light.

eight

# Sunrise

Under a flax-coloured sky, Pedra Branca is aglow. It is resplendent as it bathes in the light. I yawn, and sit up. The barking of seals cavorting off the rocky shoreline below has woken me. It's no dream, then, for here I am. I have slept and woken on a rock shelf, on a deserted island off the coast of Southern Tasmania. I am alone and without a vessel. The gods will have to align if I am to hitch a lift home today.

The sky lightens and the horizon glows as, shakily, I get to my feet and look around. I am sure the albatross I saw was also real – the experience as vivid as it had been soothing – but nonetheless I fail to see any recent evidence of a bird on the ledge. Birdlife, however, is abundant. As the new day dawns, large flocks dip and weave around the rocky peaks above me. The clouds have cleared and there is little wind, but the swell is large in the aftermath of the storm.

With eyes cast to sea, I strain to look beyond the swell and across the vast ocean. There is no rescue craft in sight, no sign at all of *Mulwala*. There are no fishing boats riding the continuum of waves that roll on and on. Pulling at my damp jacket, I manage to drag it off me. Immediately, the cold seeps in and I wonder if I am premature in my actions. *Should I wait for the sun to rise higher*? Too late now; I won't be wearing a wet coat.

My clothes are drenched, they smell disgusting, are uncomfortable and restrict me in their soggy state. Layer by layer I shed boating garb; my stiffened limbs slow to obey as the pile of discarded clothing steadily grows. I inspect the evidence of my previous day's ordeal, purple bruising a vivid reminder of scrambling to shore. My hands, knees, elbows, and stomach are grazed, and I have a gash on my hip. Opening the grab bag, I dig around until I feel the thermal underwear sensibly stored with our emergency supplies. In haste, I pull it on. It feels good to be dry, despite the woollen underwear being Sam's old thermals and a little on the large side.

I eat another muesli bar and ration myself to a few squares of chocolate. I drink a third of the bottle of water before realising how much I've guzzled. Reminding myself of how important it is to ration my supplies, I continue searching through the grab bag, looking for the EPIRB. Beads of sweat break out on my forehead as I snatch back a flare that rolls dangerously close to the edge of my rocky ledge. It had escaped from the pile of items I had pushed against the shelf wall. I continue to rifle through, even though I know we failed to put it in. I panic. The EPIRB is not there. 'Argh!'

I remember asking Sam why the EPIRB was loose in the locker. 'I threw a few treats in the bag and then I got sidetracked,' he'd said.

'Well, sort it before we set sail, or it's another job I'll have to do,' I'd replied, frustrated.

'Don't throw out any of the chocolate.'

I could never stay cross at him. His easy-going ways made me smile. I didn't even think about the bag again until *Mulwala* went down and I was fleeing for my life. I got the emergency bag but failed to reach for the EPIRB.

Collapsing onto my knees, I look towards the mainland. *So close.* If I strain my eyes, I can see the faintest outline of land in the morning glare. Leaving the EPIRB in the locker wasn't our only mistake. Sam and I had not registered our departure with Tas Maritime radio. It had been a conscious decision. I wipe sweat off my brow with an angry sweep of my hand. I always notified Tas Maritime of our trips. This was my job, not Sam's.

Sam and I were fleeing from summer festivities, work on charter boats, and tourists and events that meant we were never free of company. Not registering our travel plans had been a deliberate oversight. We were exhausted of social skills and desperate for time out. We were just heading to the southernmost bay on Bruny Island and staying in sheltered waters, or so we had told ourselves. We wanted to get lost for a few days. How ironic.

I sink back onto the shelf and curl up, pulling the thermal blanket around me. I can't believe it. The more I berate myself the more I cry, self-pity biting me harder than the cold rock on which I lie.

An hour passes, maybe more. I don't know. The warmth of the sun finally gives me cause to stir. I walk to the edge of the ledge. Turning towards the rock, I tilt my head back, and look for a path to lead me upwards. Researchers apparently access the top of the island from this point. There must be a way up. As I step towards the northern end of the ledge, I see a small cairn, perhaps a trail. And after a few paces further, I stop.

'There it is!' I shout with relief.

It's a crack in the rock; then another. I should be able to find footholds.

I secure the hastily repacked grab bag. With a few flares in hand, just in case, I take my first tentative steps upwards. My boat shoes provide good grip in weathered grooves and my confidence grows. On a larger ledge, about halfway up from the shelf, I see a series of smaller ledges to the west. My hands are raw, with shredded knuckles, but the going is easier here and I can step upwards without using them.

It's not long before I stand atop the northern end of Pedra. The exertion has been good for me. It's cleared my head and loosened tight muscles. The sun is shining, fluffy clouds benign. But exposed to the elements, I am quickly cooled by the morning breeze when I stop moving. I slap my arms and legs before turning slowly. Wide-eyed, I take in my first full view of the island and what is beyond. The movement of the sea is animated in the aftermath of the storm front, and swell laps hungrily at Pedra's sides. It is unnerving to see waves sweep up and onto the rocky ramp upon which I had sought refuge only yesterday. I scan the sea and the sky. With neither boats nor planes to be seen, I have no need of flares.

To the east, the sun has risen well above the horizon. Its warmth is a gift. Above me, a low saddle in the humped back of Pedra lies in early morning shadow. Beyond, the highest vantage point of the island is mauve and ochre in the morning light. The guano below my feet is testimony to the number of birds that have visited this rock over many years.

Shivering, I repeatedly stomp my feet, trying to keep warm. I get my bearings and continue my appraisal of Pedra. To the east stands Eddystone Rock a few kilometres away. Towering abruptly, Eddystone reaches thirty metres above the water's surface. The sharp, rocky tower is hard to miss. Sunlight catches spray from waves that crack with force against her sheer walls. Gannets bravely nosedive for their breakfast and gulls circle.

As I retrace my steps and descend from the summit, I am surprised by how agile I am despite my injuries. Many years of daily exercises have put me in good stead. I'm grateful that my injuries are not incapacitating, but to stay in good shape I need to keep moving.

Back at my temporary home base, I attempt a few star jumps. My clothes are yet to dry and keeping warm until they do will give me focus. As I start to do a few side-to-side stretches, a memory of standing in front of an aerobics class in the mid-eighties flashes across my mind. I was living in Hong Kong at the time. How my classes would laugh if they could see me in my oversized thermals doing a version of the grapevine on an isolated rock in the Southern Ocean. How surprising to remember such things, and at such a time. The mind is good at distraction when distraction is easier than facing reality.

Hong Kong was not a destination of choice for me. Cities don't motivate me. Being raised in the country, I prefer wide open spaces. I feel confined and claustrophobic in cities. When I have space around me, breathing becomes easier. My then-husband – and father of my children, Matt and Sasha – had been working for a Melbourne-based company. He was asked to move to Hong Kong to update a computer banking system. Matt and Sasha were young children at the time. I agreed to the move so that our family was not divided.

Our time in this vibrant, crowded city was to affect both my son and daughter in a myriad of ways, as it did me. Aerobics instructors on the island were in short supply then, so I had plenty of work. It helped me to cope with the absence of life as I knew it in Australia, the absence of greenery, and the vacant space growing in my heart. Adaptation is a useful survival tool.

I wipe my hands over my face, then pull my shoulders back. It's time to evaluate and plan for a stay on Pedra for at least a day or two, my estimation of the time it would take for family to alert the authorities that Sam and I were missing. I must, one: stay positive; two: stick to rationed food and ensure I have water; and, three: dry my clothes. Come nightfall, I will need warmth. I'm not in Hong Kong now. The nights are long and cold in Tasmania. Sunlight fully bathes the ledge and I take a moment to lift my face towards the warmth. Carefully upending the grab bag, I examine the precious contents, one by one.

Without the thermal blanket, I am unsure if I would have survived the storm last night. The sun has now dried it nicely, and I fold it up before placing it aside. Thermal blankets have twice before helped to save me from hypothermia; once as a skinny teenager in Victoria's high country, and then a year later in a snowstorm in New Zealand. My mind is intent on going down memory lane. I wonder if this is a subconscious survival strategy.

The sun caresses me as I sit cross-legged, laying out the contents of the grab bag. I place the four flares, first-aid kit, waterproof matches, pocketknife, and duct tape to one side for the time being. As well as the block of Cadbury chocolate, there is a bag of white chocolate-covered raspberries, my favourites. The food stash is completed with a packet of Minties and several more muesli bars. I don't know whether to curse Sam or send him silent thanks, but sustenance from these goodies may just enhance my chances of survival. Without the treats, though, an EPIRB would have easily slid into the bag. When I next see Sam, I won't know whether to embrace him or slap him.

A fluffing sound, much like when a doona is shaken, startles me. There to my right is the albatross. I freeze. It looks at me warily. I'm afraid to breathe yet am thrilled to see this magnificent bird again. It is a Shy Albatross – known to frequent Pedra Branca – with its yellow beak tilted towards me. I recall reading about this albatross and being saddened by the decline of the species. It breeds on three Tasmanian islands only and competes with gannets for nesting space. Longline fishing has taken its toll on bird numbers.

'Were you hurt in the storm, my friend?'

Very slowly, I reach my hand towards the bird. A few crumbs rest on my palm.

It eyes me warily but maintains eye contact.

'What shall we call you then? I think Eva suits. How does that sound to you, Eva?'

Moments pass.

'It's okay, Eva. I'm your friend.'

Eva hops towards me, hooded eyes scrutinising me over a sloping beak. I don't flinch as she tilts her head towards my hand. A quick movement and the crumbs are gone. For a bird named for its shyness, this albatross is very inquisitive. She fluffs her wings and I see fishing line constricting the mid part of one wing, at the joint.

'Oh, you poor thing!' I exclaim, frightening Eva.

She flaps her wings and backs away from me. The bird is nearly at the edge of the shelf before she takes flight. One wing dips a little below the other as the albatross steadily climbs in height, then flies towards the southern end of the island. How I want to help her; how I long for her to stay close to me.

Devastated, I shudder uncontrollably, the thermal blanket shaken from my shoulders. Great sobs from somewhere deep inside erupt with ferocity. With my body heaving, I howl my lonely grief to the wind and sea. I grieve for the bird, fearing she will not survive. I'm crying for me, too. I have lost my soulmate, *Mulwala* – my home – and I may well lose myself on this remote and isolated island.

Nature has given me what few people have: a sense of security, of belonging, and belief. Loneliness is a different thing and something I have fought before. And then I met Sam. It was Sam who shook me out of myself, Sam who bought a yacht and asked me to live aboard with him, and it was Sam who became my companion in boating, hiking, and life adventures. Since my children left home – independence encouraged, but loss still felt – I had not known such easy companionship. Sam was like a soft jumper, worn close. Now he has left me adrift.

'Sam, where are you?' I whisper to the breeze.

Bereft, I look southwards, willing Eva to reappear. I gaze out to sea and watch gulls settle expertly atop waves and adjust to the swell. A seal pops up below me – closer to the island than the masses – and as I watch he flips over, fans the air with his flippers and, content with conditions, sunbakes. Seals are a resilient sea mammal and always seem to be at ease in their surrounds, no matter what the conditions.

*Take heed, Kay.*

Clouds are building once more, rays of light tearing at their fabric and creating fans of gold that stretch to the sea. I think of the albatross.

*Please heal Eva; don't give up.*

I rest my head on my repacked bag of supplies with clothes strewn around me as they dry. I'm spent. Loneliness tests us. We can succumb to it or find a way to accept it and move forward. Closing my eyes, I swallow back emotions, breathe deeply, and will negative thoughts to fly away with the clouds.

nine
# Camino de Santiago

I was living in Melbourne in 2002 when an Irish neighbour, of Derry origin, told me about a trek across Spain. Sean was a natural and compelling storyteller. He fed me tales of the Camino and the enlightenment, both spiritual and otherwise, experienced by those who embarked on the pilgrimage. It was then that I decided to tackle the Camino de Santiago. Life had recently thrown me a few curve balls; I was lonely, and I craved distraction. Much to Sean's surprise and my own, I decided I would start training and tackle the Camino de Santiago that very year.

I forewent the hiking boots and found myself a second-hand pushbike to satisfy my newfound zest for cycling. It was an old steel road bike equipped with a set of panniers. My training was intensive. I did a lot of riding over the next few months, including some intense training rides in the Dandenong Ranges. Every Saturday for months prior, I clipped into my bike pedals and made the three-hour round trip into the city from my suburban home. I would spend the mornings working at a bike store, learning all I could about maintaining and repairing bikes. I was on my way to France to begin my pilgrimage not more than four months later.

Along with Rome and Jerusalem, the Camino de Santiago is one of the most significant Christian pilgrimages of the

Middle Ages. My motivation was not of a religious nature, but for enlightenment of sorts. I was soul searching, then. Seeking physical beauty, challenge and solitude – I speak neither French nor Spanish – I hoped to ultimately discover the peace of mind I longed for. Being outdoors and exercising, with the sensory delights of the environment inspiring me, would bring clarity and perspective, reason would be restored, and my own company better tolerated; or so I had hoped.

Arriving in Paris, I breakfasted at a café on the Champs-Élysées. Dappled sunlight dropped like jewels into my glass of sparkling water. Nearby lovers held hands while sharing a croissant. It was the first day of summer in a perfect setting. Paris, city of romance, enticed me with sunlight, succulent market strawberries, lush breads, rich coffee and flirtatious Frenchmen. It was a far cry from my Australian experiences where certain men might consider wolf whistles and a slap on the bottom a sufficient, perhaps economical way to attract a woman. In France, however, men would flirt with subtle charm. Doors were opened for me, graciousness extended, meals placed before me with elegant flair and smiles dispensed with a discreet nod of the head. There is a fine art to flirting and the attention helped to divert my gaze from the fact that I was embarking on a solitary, and what was sure to be arduous, adventure.

Didier, a French friend I had met hiking in Tasmania, had agreed to meet my train in Cannes after I travelled from Paris. I was delighted to accept the offer of accommodation at his apartment in Grasse, twenty-five kilometres inland from the Mediterranean. Here I would rest up before my ride, explore the village and prepare for the journey ahead. Some years prior, Didier and his then-partner had stayed at my home in Melbourne, and I had taken on the role of host and tour guide. One of the joys of travelling is meeting different people and the joy is doubled when catching up with those same people in their own country. Didier was an excellent host.

After stashing my bike and luggage in his van and donning swimsuits, Didier and I dove into the deliciously warm Mediterranean and swam far out from shore. As we floated, my friend pointed in the direction of nearby Italy, Monaco, Spain, the Alps and the hills of Grasse. Later, narrow streets with stone walls led us up a steep hill above the village of Grasse to Didier's enchanting apartment. We ate pasta, cooked by Didier and made with local ingredients, drank excellent red wine and toasted our renewed acquaintance across a wine barrel, complete with tablecloth and candles. Ah, the French! I was seduced in more ways than one. The view from the deck, over the valley and beyond to the Mediterranean, was breathtaking. A twelfth-century church close by tolled the hour, the ringing of the bell reverberating long over the lush vales. From Didier's bedroom window, a vista of palms, cypresses and other conifers provided a green foreground to a most beautiful country.

Fortified by good food and good company, I began my bike ride at Arles, taking off on one of the oldest traditional routes for the pilgrimage, and from what had once been the home of Vincent van Gogh. I was to stand on the same cobblestones on which he had stood. A local painter I met at a fruit market gave me a brief tour, pointing out the building where van Gogh had lived. I stood beneath the bedroom window through which van Gogh had gazed at the night sky. I began my pilgrimage at a point in my life where I was struggling with inner demons, just as van Gogh was when he looked to the stars above Arles for inspiration.

Generosity and warmth do not need words. A monk was to meet me at the Arles train station before commencing my ride and despite the language barrier, I knew I was being wished luck on my pilgrimage and blessed by the monk as he placed a booklet in my hands. Didier had arranged for this. As I pedalled along the dedicated Camino route, I stopped at various destinations and had my book signed by monks, as tradition entailed.

In truth, I did feel watched over from that point on. Later that same day, after getting stumped at the outset by my poor sense of direction, I made it to Saint Giles, my first official stop over. Here a solicitous, elderly French lady led me to a seldom-used refuge for pilgrims. We negotiated narrow wooden steps on the outside of a building to reach a small space under a pigeon coop. This lovely lady had cleaned the area and arranged a bed, beside which she had placed a small table, adorned with a jar of wildflowers.

On each day of the seven weeks of my pilgrimage from Arles to Santiago, I faced new challenges. The rewards equalled the magnitude of each challenge. Sometimes the going was tough; sometimes the beauty of the landscape so overwhelmed me that I sang. And I sang loudly, my voice curling around the vines in the endless vineyards and disappearing into the deep hues of the mountainous background.

Another time I was besieged by bed bugs in a shabby hotel where guests were treated as friends. And it was here that I was invited to an outdoor family picnic. Trestle tables covered in tablecloths were laden with food, as ancient trees spread limbs of thick foliage to protect us from the harsh midday sun. I recall an afternoon with much-needed company, merriment, and respite. As the sun burned itself out in the still of the evening, I fell into my bed, sated and happy. But no sooner had I turned out the light than bed bugs besieged me. I spent the best part of that night in a bath where I gained at least some relief from unbearable itchiness. There was a lesson to be learnt from my stay at that hotel, and it seemed to me that it was to enjoy the good and accept the bad. To do so is to make the best choice when choices are few.

Embracing the highs and lows of my adventure was a prerequisite for success. This was easier said than done, but I tried. At times I was desperate, lonely, and at other times so exhausted I felt a danger on the roads and actually baulked at the effort more than once, throwing the bike on a bus for short distances. It takes practice to become a good pilgrim.

There was neither the need nor the energy for soul searching. Nature provided and I revelled in the moment. In Spain I felt joy, the strong bonds of family and the strength of communities. Spaniards are survivors; the brutal battles between the Christians and the Moors are legendary and had a lasting impact on the people. I absorbed the prevalent air of an enduring populace and landscape. As my quadriceps developed and my bike shorts stretched, so too did my inner strength grow. There were times during my pilgrimage when I felt like quitting, yet never seriously entertained the thought. I would keep riding until I reached Santiago. I would not quit. That same resolve, bolstered by my experiences on the Camino, was to become more pronounced as the years passed. Knowing when to rest, recuperate and take stock would take me much longer to learn. Life's balance is not easily managed.

The exhaustion I felt pedalling over the Pyrenees to reach Spain surpassed anything I had previously experienced. My true limits were tested and yet I endured. Riding out of Astorga, finally in the hills again after vast distances of dry, flat, hot expanses, I rejoiced. Even approaching the dreaded Foncebadón (I had read accounts of wild, unfriendly dogs who had taken over this practically deserted mountain village) I kept my head down and bottom up. I attempted to portray a confident air. I was unduly rewarded by grinning dogs that stretched lazily in the shade of crumbling rock walls.

I kept pedalling. I had a long, steep climb ahead of me before I reached my next stop, El Acebo. Perched on a steep, thirty-degree incline, El Acebo is a small village of slate-roofed houses with wooden balconies. That day I reached new personal limits, riding mostly uphill for 140 kilometres. There is no doubt that I should have rested after my epic push to El Acebo. Instead, I chose to go on the next day, adrenaline propelling me towards the walled village of O'Cebreiro. I had ridden seventeen days straight at that point in time. My drive was similar to a mountain climber's obsession; I chose to go on when instincts screamed at me to stop.

There was no turning back when a summer storm darkened the sky and quickly became ferocious, plunging me into a pit of despair. I was a mere seventy kilometres from my destination, Santiago. I had anticipated contending with the dry summer heat, not pushing a bike up a mountain with visibility lost in a sea of impenetrable cloud while under relentless attack from an angry black sky that spat rain like bullets and roared as if possessed. My bike shoes slipped out of the bike cleats on steep, wet terrain, so I took them off and continued on in sodden socks, lightning and thunder my companions under an impenetrable cloud. The road to the village is exposed and is known to have some of the harshest weather in Spain.

The storm howled, the intensity of which was unrelenting. The mind takes over when the body is spent. I pushed and pedalled up the barren road, with no place to hide, lightning dancing in frantic activity across the peaks, wind weaving cold bands around me and rain lashing from all directions, stinging like a wet towel whipping. I was utterly alone and felt the cloying hands of death teasing and enticing me.

I almost gave way to despair on that mountain, engulfed in darkness, wanting to disappear, willing an end to the nightmare. My body and mind were taxed to the point where I considered the easiest option: to simply fall off the side of the mountain into oblivion. I was wrecked. During that long day, as nature threw its worst at me, it was as if life had led me to that critical point. The decision was mine, fight or die. For a while, dying seemed easier.

Eventually, my hand touched the cold stone walls of the mountain hamlet. With the cloud as dense as porridge wrapping itself around the mountain, I felt, rather than saw, my way along the rough wall until I found the entrance to O'Cebreiro. Collapsing onto a step, rain unheeded, I let my bike fall. I was vaguely aware of feet passing by me going up or down the steps. I have no idea how much time passed before a warm hand reached out to me and I was led into a pilgrim *albergue*, or *refugio*. Shattered, having been all but bereft of hope, I had made it to the gateway of northern Galicia. Somehow, I had lived. I was to learn one of life's greatest lessons from that experience, a lesson that would take me years to fully appreciate. No matter how bleak the day, after darkness there will always be light.

ten

# The cave

Sitting on a slab of rock a long way from anywhere and with no means of getting to or communicating with the world beyond Pedra Branca, I assess my situation. The odds are not stacked in my favour. In order to survive, I need to believe that I can; I must know that I will.

I cross my legs, rest my upturned palms on my knees and, raising my face to the sun, take in several deep, cleansing breaths.

'Om mani padme hum. Om mani padme hum.'

The mantra is calming, and I give my mind free rein.

Bright light penetrates my eyelids as I imagine Sam before me, his arms open as I fall into him, emotional respite, and the strength of his belief in me bolstering me anew. As far as tests go, this is the ultimate. The Camino de Santiago was a tough journey, and yet I had survived and did so on my own. That was long before I met Sam.

*I can do this; I just have to believe that I can.*

I continue to sit, letting thoughts flow as they will, the sun on my body and Sam in my heart.

With the sun now high and my clothes dry I dress briskly, intent on moving beyond my base and exploring the island further. Carefully choosing items to take with me, I push a couple of flares into my coat pocket. I empty a large zip lock bag of notepad and pencil. *I'll use this as a water bladder,* I think as I put the bag into another pocket. Finally, I reach into the grab bag for a snack and the multipurpose knife Sam had bought me for my last birthday, which I have yet to use. I do a couple of quick stretches and despite muscles that are calling out for a soft bed, start making my way to the southern end of the island. Although the swell is still large, the day is clear and calm. Waves undulate, full and fat under an expansive blue sky, clouds few and scattered. The weather looks to be improving. I need to take full advantage of the conditions.

The worst-case scenario, I tell myself, is that help is up to three days away. Given the storm last night and the fact that, unless Sam has notified the authorities, an alert of missing persons may not be given for a couple of days, my first priorities are water and shelter. Rationing my water won't be easy. I'm already running low. Shading my eyes with my hand, I look for a way to safely navigate across the rough terrain.

It is tough going and the rocks are becoming more uneven as I pick my way forward. Crawling hand over foot, being sure of where I place my feet and aiming to employ the boatie's safety principle of three points of contact with a surface, progress is slow. As my dad would say, 'Better safe than sorry.' The weather could deteriorate again, another storm could hit. This may be my only chance of searching for water and a sturdier shelter, so I persevere. In the distance, I think I see a depression below the steep southern point of Pedra. I have read of a cave on the southern end of the island. *Where is the entrance?*

Resting for a few moments, I watch as gulls circle overhead and Black-faced Cormorant's perch in stately fashion on pointy outcrops, wings draped wide to dry. Cormorants have an uncanny diving accuracy. They can dive in water to around forty metres and hold their breath for up to sixty seconds, ensuring that they have a good success rate when fishing. Sure enough, a cormorant emerges from the water below me with a decent-sized meal in its beak. Waterbirds have been my constant companions in the time I've lived on a boat, both in the marina and cruising Tasmanian waterways. Watching them is familiar and comforting. I remember seeing a massive flock of shearwaters yesterday, just before nightfall, hundreds and hundreds of them flying low over the water as they emerged from the south, wing tips almost skimming the water as they flew in perfect unity. Aware now that the sun is getting higher in the sky, I scramble resolutely onwards.

I reach the southern end of the island after a few hours of wearying focus. Sitting for a few moments, I reflect on what an imposing island Pedra Branca is. She may be small, but she is, nonetheless, a mighty chunk of rock in a vast and unpredictable ocean. This rock has saved my life thus far and, as dire as my circumstances might be, I feel a strong sense of connection to her. Funny that I think of Pedra as 'her', as we do boats. Likewise, I named the albatross Eva. Perhaps the feminine connotation is a reference to that which helps us feel secure.

And just as a mother opens her arms to provide comfort, suddenly Pedra reveals to me a place of shelter. The cave entrance! I crouch down ready to enter the dimly lit cave. I pause on the threshold to let my eyesight adjust to the dark interior, only to jump backwards in surprise when I realise that I'm not alone. As my heart rate steadies, I study the albatross. She stands against the cave wall, eyeing me in turn.

It's Eva. There is no mistaking her mismatched wings, one tilting slightly lower than the other. I wish I had some crumbs in my pocket. I'm scared I will frighten the bird. Sudden movement could exacerbate her injury. I ease my back against the cave wall and slowly slide into a squatting position. Eva does not move. I sit for several minutes, surprised that she is not reacting more fearfully.

Sick or injured birds and animals often seek safe and quiet places to heal, and I suspect the albatross has sought to rest in this cave. After long minutes of appraisal, during which time Eva does little more than tilt her head from side to side, I make some slight movements of adjustment.

'It's okay. I won't hurt you, Eva,' I murmur quietly, as I carefully inch my way towards her.

Eva stares at my progress, transfixed.

'You are a clever bird, finding this shelter.'

Eva lifts her head and I stop, bending my knees so that we are on the same level. The cave is not large and has a low ceiling. The Shy Albatross can grow up to ninety centimetres in height, and, as I guess Eva to be a mature bird, I estimate the ceiling height to be double that. I look around me. There, close to Eva, is a small pool of water. It looks clean, fed by rain collecting at the cave's entrance. Seeing the precious water, I silently rejoice. Eva has chosen her sanctuary wisely.

I continue to inch my way towards her. Finally, I am mere feet away. Our eye contact has not faltered. Dark eyes, set deep, seem to penetrate me. Regal over a long, sloping beak, she holds my gaze and simultaneously fluffs out her wings. I see the fishing line I glimpsed earlier.

'It's okay, it's okay,' I say in a whisper, backing off a little and once more sinking to the ground.

Normally albatross fly with effortless ease. This fishing line is clearly the reason Eva lacks the usual finesse of these beautiful sea birds. It is wrapped around the middle joint of Eva's wing and looks to have pulled tight. I hate to see one of these rare birds injured in its natural environment. Once harvested for meat, feathers, and eggs, breeding pairs are slowly on the incline again, despite their vulnerability to human activities such as commercial fishing.

*What are my chances?* I think as I prepare myself. I flick open the multipurpose knife and examine the tools it offers.

A serrated blade might do the trick. I worry that I could hurt her, but what choice do I have? She will likely suffer, more surely die if I leave her tangled, the line impeding her ability to fly. Inching with care towards the albatross, I gingerly reach out my free hand, as I had when I offered her food. She withdraws from me, flapping around the cave. Retreating, I rest on my haunches and barely breathe as I wait for her to calm.

Surprisingly, she does not try to leave the cave. She stops hopping about and lets her wings drop. I guess she is asking me to slow down, give her time to adjust. Eva settles and I resume talking quietly, attempting to reassure her. I'm talking to an albatross and she's *listening*. Cocking her head, Eva gazes at me with curiosity. Anger wells within me as I think of how careless people can be with their fishing practices and dumping of rubbish into the sea, without consideration for all the sea life and birds that know the ocean as their home.

Getting as close as I dare, I reach out for a second time. Eva does not retreat. My fingers touch the bird's wing. I withdraw, sitting again, talking quietly all the while. The next time I reach out, she lets my fingers linger on her silky feathers and, seemingly frozen, does not adjust her position. Incredible as it is, I may have gained a degree of trust from this magnificent bird. If it is stress that has induced immobility, it might work to my advantage. I don't want Eva to stress more, so it's now or never. I reach forward and position the blade close to the wing, continuing my hushed monotone monologue. I hold my breath as I ease the blunted edge of the serrated blade under the fishing line then twist it swiftly, pulling it up and away from her wing, slicing the line cleanly. Eva hops back from me, emitting a guttural cackling sound.

'Wow, we did it!' I am delighted. Eva continues to hop around, stretching her wings wide. The fishing line has fallen cleanly off her wing and lies on the floor of the cave. Joy floods through me. With the wing now free, she bows her head and looks to where the joint was once bound. With dignified grace, Eva raises both wings evenly, exercising her joints in front of me before she puffs out her chest, proud and free.

eleven
# White feathers

The sun slides into the sea, creating a luminescent sheen. Striated clouds, indigo, stretch long arms, and the vast Southern Ocean melts into a red horizon. My legs are heavy and slow as I near my base on the rock shelf. Pausing, I sip precious water I collected from the cave's rock pool and nibble on chocolate, savouring each square. It had been hard to leave Eva. Loneliness is not my friend.

I look up towards the highest point on the island, mentally checking the route I plan to take to get to the northern summit. Having already walked up to the point, I can more readily make out the path. I should make it back down before nightfall. I feel for the small torch that I keep in the inside pocket of my jacket. Although I have resolved to go up to my lookout point morning and night to check for any boats or planes, it takes a lot of willpower to pick my legs up again. I think of Eva and her bravery, and try to find motivation. I am so bloody tired; all I want to do is curl up in a ball and sleep.

The sunset is intense and the view breathtaking from the summit of Pedra. It's as if a golden carpet has been thrown over the water, so perfect is the colour of the sky reflected in the sea. There is no boat, nor plane, to be seen. I am acutely aware of how small, how easy to miss I am; a mere speck on a tiny island, in a vast ocean, below a big sky. I collapse onto my knees and weep.

I am knackered as I arrive back at my camp from the lookout. I sit heavily, head in my hands, scratched, torn inside and out, and so hungry my stomach cramps painfully. So much for all the positive self-talk. I keep telling myself to be tough, that I will endure, but it is getting harder all the time to be confident of rescue. It has been days – how many I cannot count at this point – since I last ate a meal. I suck in air and wish it was liquid. I know I need to eat something, but the effort to reach for my meagre food supplies is too much and the food I do have too little. With shaking hands, I manage to open the grab bag and tear the wrapping on a muesli bar. Swallowing is difficult, despite my hunger. I must be a bit dehydrated. Sipping water between mouthfuls of food, I see the first star of the night appear.

As each new star pretties the sky and I chew methodically, I draw on images of meals I will eat when I get back home. Breakfast first. It is my favourite meal of the day. I close my eyes and see a pot of tea in front of me, a whole pot, and a large bowl of porridge, honey dissolving as I pour milk on top. I can smell it; steamy sweetened oats. I'd follow this down with thick slices of toast covered in lashings of butter and jam. Craving carbohydrates, I can literally feel myself diminishing. My hand snakes out to retrieve a chocolate bar.

Lightheaded from hunger and exertion, I lay my meagre food rations at my feet and mentally divide it up according to the worst-case scenario I can imagine – that it will be three days until I am rescued. I could eat everything before me in minutes and am salivating with longing, but the satisfaction would be short-lived if my food supplies are then naught. I forcibly hold my hands together, digging my nails into my palms to stop myself from eating more. The agony of seeing food I cannot immediately eat is torture and I shove my rations back in the bag.

At least I have water now, and I know where to find more if I need it. Eva had sat quietly while I first tested the pool of water, my head close to her pink-tinged webbed feet across the puddle. Collecting the water in the zip lock bag had been challenging, and I had resorted to using my mouth as a scoop of sorts. What Eva thought of my behaviour, I can only guess. Perhaps she had been tolerant of me because I resembled a mother bird, sourcing sustenance before returning to her nest to feed young.

I fold the high-vis sheet in half and then in half again, positioning myself on it to protect myself from the cold stone underneath. Made of PVC, the sheet may not be a soft couch, however it does provide valuable insulation between myself and the cold rock. I wrap the thermal blanket around my body, tucking in every corner as the evening chill sends a shiver down my spine. The flares are close by and easily reachable. I curl into a ball, dragging the blanket with me. I'm shaking from hunger or exhaustion, I'm not sure which. I pull the blanket over my head.

The closest point on the Tasmanian mainland is little more than twenty nautical miles from me and could be reached by boat in half a day in the right conditions. So near and yet so far.

*Please God, don't leave me here for too much longer.*

Nature is my god. Am I praying to Mother Nature?

*I'm going bonkers.*

I pray regardless.

Eyelids fluttering, I think of Eva. I pray for a return to full health for her and an imminent rescue for me. I pray for a reunion with my children, family, and with Sam. The immense lure of sleep is hard to fight and as I lose the tug-of-war between wakefulness and sweet oblivion, I pray I see a boat on the horizon when next I open my eyes.

I dream. High-speed imagery – like in David Attenborough documentaries – thrusts the humped shoulders of a mountain upwards from the bottom of the ocean. This land mass will be known as Pedra Branca. As it unfolds and emerges resplendent from the sea, it shrugs off water in giant waves. With volcanic force the island erupts, spewing birds from its core. Dramatic rumblings disturb the ocean floor, causing Pedra to spit and splutter for many days, sending thousands upon thousands of feathers shooting upwards in a white plume. The volcano calms as the island becomes fully formed, claiming independence from mainland Tasmania, to which it was once connected by tenuous threads. The feathers settle in a neat line created by tide and current.

A single surviving bird, a Shy Albatross, flies effortlessly across the sea, following a bridge of white feathers that mark the way from the island to the mainland. I step forth and start to run along the feathery trail, following the albatross, going faster and faster, crying out, arms opened.

twelve
# The albatross

A light breeze pulls at my blanket, which crackles like aluminium foil, and I am momentarily surprised not to feel the softness of my doona. I pull it more closely around myself regardless, trying to ward off the early morning chill and the bite of reality. My eyes open. I look to the north. There is no bridge. It was but a dream. A lovely dream. I close my eyes again to delay confronting another day on Pedra Branca.

Burying my head down inside the neck of my jacket, I am grateful for the warmth it provides. I think of the cave where I would be assured shelter, and perhaps companionship. Sheltering in the cave would be a last resort, however, because I need to be in the open and visible. The sensation of warm breath rising up around my cheeks and ears gives me small pleasure. Listening, I hear waves breaking on Pedra's shores, seals barking and raucous birds crying out for breakfast. Another day. I pray it is the day I will be rescued.

Body reluctant, I push myself into a sitting position, hungrily reaching for a muesli bar. Everything is getting harder. It's harder to stay positive; harder to keep disciplined about food rationing. Looking out across the ocean all is calm, swell noticeably diminished and the dusty pink of sunrise a memory on the horizon. Below me, waves curl up onto the base of Pedra, ebbing and flowing, having an easy day.

I lean forward and turn to take in as much of the ocean as I can, still unwilling to stand, sleep heavy. How I long to see a boat come into view. I look upwards, craning my neck to see the vantage point I had scrambled to last night. Not a bad effort after a long day. To do it again this morning will require energy that is increasingly difficult to summon. Wary of standing too quickly as I'm a little light-headed, I gingerly roll over. Needing to pee, I haul myself up to a standing position and walk tentatively across the shelf before pulling down my pants to urinate. Reasoning it will take less energy not to fully squat, I put my hands on my knees, peeing on the rock in a semi-upright position. Not a splash, but a dribble. I am dehydrated. My head spins and I feel myself pitching forward, only narrowly avoiding falling flat on my face.

*Whoa, that was too close for comfort.*

I stay on my hands and knees until the dizziness passes.

Crawling to the back of the shelf, I reach for the water bottle and swallow several big mouthfuls. My lips are swollen and cracked, and it hurts to drink. Once I am steadier, I stand and lean against the rock wall. I flex my toes and feet, shake out my legs, roll my shoulders, then stretch my arms overhead. It helps to alleviate the wobbles, but I know my strength is waning. Breakfast does not consist of tea and porridge; what I have will have to suffice. It's food, and I need the calories to get safely to the lookout again. The white chocolate covered raspberries are the best treat (both delicious and reminding me that Sam is with me, somehow) and I put a few in my pocket for the walk to the lookout. Firstly, I have to summon the energy to do so. Keeping vigil is a priority, as I may have but one chance of rescue.

I nearly choke on my chocolate when I hear a flap of wings close by. Turning, I see Eva has landed several feet away. How extraordinary that she has come back to me. My smile pulls at the cracks on my lips and I wince. I strain to look closely at

Eva, alert for any sign of lingering injury. As if giving answer to an unspoken question, she fluffs out her wings before settling quietly.

'You're looking good,' I exclaim joyfully.

Eva tilts her head to one side with an air of patient expectancy. Her dark brow twitches. I stretch out my arm and open my hand in a silent offering, revealing a few chocolate crumbs. The bird remains motionless. I shuffle forward, inch by inch, until I am close enough to reach out and touch Eva. She snatches the crumbs from my hand in one swift movement, leans back, then settles on the rock once more.

We have breakfast together, Eva and I, quietly and without fuss, looking out over the Southern Ocean and sharing our meagre meal. She is the excuse I need to eat the remaining portion of my muesli bar and several chocolates, deviating from my rationing. As crumbs scatter, the bird hops around me, so close that I feel feathers brush against me. Reaching into the water bladder, I cup a little of the liquid in my palm and moisten my lips, before offering Eva a drink. The taste is a little stale and slightly metallic but I am confident it is clean and drinkable after the recent rain. I have little choice regardless. As I hold my hand steady Eva is tentative at first and then, to my delight, she drinks.

Above us birds come and go, gannets, cormorants, albatross, and gulls alighting on Pedra's rocky summits with breakfast in their beaks for waiting chicks. It is as if, now that the storm has passed and weather has settled, life on Pedra resumes normality for those that call this island home. Chicks in their nests, protected in the cracks and crevices of Pedra Branca, need to be fed as they will fledge soon. There is a sense of busyness on Pedra as the sun rises and the colour and activity on the island escalates.

With the rock as my backrest, I watch as sea-birds dive with precision. They surface from the water cleanly, small fish in their beaks. Seagulls crowd and squabble, as they do wherever they are in the world. Larger pacific gulls with their bulbous orange beaks weave around the island, lacing through the throng, on the lookout for unguarded offerings. They have to be quick before others dive on their target. I too would provide competition for a feed of fish if I had a fishing line. I hug my arms over my stomach; hunger gnaws. I tell myself I will head to the lookout shortly.

My thoughts turn to Sam and to my children. I speak quietly to Eva, who is beside me now, confiding how much I long to hug those I love and to be hugged in turn. My feathered friend tilts her head from side to side, hooded eyes gauging me over her long, sloping beak. She is a regal-looking bird. I keep talking, warming up now, the albatross an attentive listener. A sigh of self-pity escapes me.

'I miss my mum. I miss my kids. I miss home.'

Eva turns her head to look out over the water, as if musing over my words. I've found a friend.

I'm feeling a bit better. A little of my load has been shared. I make sure to take my time as I pack up my blanket and food securely, Eva looking on. I stretch, sunlight soothing on my face, morning rays reaching out to warm me. Focusing on my balance, I attempt a morning yoga routine, a long-practiced discipline. Only today my body refuses to cooperate and I have to keep both feet firmly on the ground. Eva is doing better than I. Unexpected laughter bubbles up within me as I watch Eva tuck one leg neatly under a wing, performing what looks like an exemplary yoga pose. I double over with mirth as the bird holds position and I am reminded what sheer delight there is to be had in a good belly laugh.

thirteen
# Alice

I was seventeen years of age when my girlfriend Leanne and I travelled to Central Australia to explore the mysteries at our country's heart. We took a bus from Melbourne to Adelaide – where it was snowing – then flew to Darwin and into oppressive humidity. After a few weeks exploring the city and surrounds, and partying nightly, we caught a tour bus which took us into Arnhem Land. The bus then travelled south on the Stuart Highway through Central Australia, and back to Adelaide.

Leanne brought a sense of fun wherever we were, be it a caravan park or a pub, livening up a crowd and leaving mirth in her wake. Once she encouraged all those in a campground for the evening to swap clothes as we partied around a campfire. For young and old travellers alike, her sense of fun was contagious.

Alice Springs in the late-seventies was stuck in prejudice, hot with injustices, and rough enough to send tourists quickly out of town. From an idyllic childhood I had emerged into a cruel teenage world and couldn't wait to leave home, start work, and make a life for myself. Not fitting in with the pack mentality, I had become a bit of a loner. My teenage years showed me that life could be tough and I had to take care of myself. New horizons were definitely on the agenda. This was to be my first independent trip away from family, and with Leanne as role model – a few years older and much savvier than I – I relearnt the art of creating fun. We got ourselves into some interesting predicaments and simply found another way of going forward as we forged friendships in unlikely places.

Geographically, Alice Springs sits roughly in the centre of the Australian mainland. Stepping inside a pub frequented by Indigenous Australians, we were not welcomed. The fault lay in the fact that most of the pubs in town had a whites-only ruling. It was a community divided. We were two inexperienced young women on an outback adventure seeking colour, flavour, and variance in the bigger world. Neither of us had travelled far from the country towns we were brought up in in Victoria, although Leanne had been more adventurous than I up until that point. Stopping to pick up a six-pack we headed to the Todd River. If we couldn't drink with the traditional custodians of this land in a bar, we would go elsewhere looking for conversation and local insights. Silver eucalyptus flanked a dry, white-sanded riverbed. Beer was welcomed by the local aboriginals who had set up camp there, and the trees stood guard while the town went about its business.

Camped on the outskirts of town, below the MacDonnell Ranges, the mood was more relaxed. In the morning sun dust created a halo above violet hills, casting a meditative spell. I went for my morning run before the heat of the day while the dogs still slept.

Someone had left a gate unlocked at the local camel farm. Before I saw the camels, I felt the stampede through my running shoes, felt the dust overtake me, grit stinging my eyeballs. Looking over my shoulder, I saw I was in the direct path of that liberated herd of beasts. Camels are intriguing animals, all gangly legs and humped backs, ferocious snorts and indignant head tilts. Most impressively, camels have the longest range of spit I had ever seen.

I leapt aside and, in my haste, inadvertently jumped into the yard of one of the shacks that were dotted along the road. An old Aboriginal fellow stood with a steaming cup of tea in a metal mug, head thrown back, laughing uproariously. I stayed for a cuppa. The mornings are cold in the outback, in rebellion against the heat of the day. Hands are warmed around mugs of hot drink, cold tinnies preferred in the afternoons. I had a good yarn with my new mate. I was becoming enamoured with Alice and the people I engaged with in this colourful part of Australia.

Evidence suggests occupation of Alice Springs by the Arrernte Aboriginal people dates back as far as 30,000 years ago. In the early 1870s, after Stuart's expedition through Central Australia revealed a crossing of the continent was possible, a telegraph station was established in Alice Springs, bringing with it a white population. I had felt like a bit of an outsider since my early years of high school. I felt an empathy with the people of this outback town, despite having little insight into the ostracism of Aboriginal people. I vowed to learn more.

Before that first adventure away from my hometown, I was cautioned about the dangers of the desert and travelling with a girlfriend only. The trip to Alice Springs not only revealed to me a fascination of outback Australia and of Indigenous culture, but it ignited in me a desire for exploration and to seek my own truths.

I was a teenager when I went to Alice Springs. Leanne taught me much just by being who she was, light-hearted, strong, open-minded, and true. She died too young, leaving a vibrant legacy. My friend's ability to reach out to others, give all who she encountered a fair go – regardless of our differences – and to laugh often and loudly, has resonated throughout my lifetime. The camel stampede may have scared the bejesus out of me, but I had survived, learnt from the experience, and made a new mate in the process.

fourteen
# Rainbow

Gulls swoop, squealing with anticipation as I unwrap a Mintie. I suck on the revitalising sweet and prepare for my climb up to the lookout. Above the water, a vigilant gull circles lower, stakes out its prey, and then dives to snatch a fish from the sea. Birds close by shriek, hoping the fish wriggles free and is an easy catch for another.

Suddenly a ball of bait fish appears and disturbs the water's surface. The fish group together in an attempt to protect themselves. From my vantage point I can clearly see that there are hundreds, if not thousands, of small fish balled up. Birds circle and dive repeatedly, and then seals are in the mix, flipping through the air as they splash and create disarray. There is frantic activity as the predators anticipate a feed. The fish stretch then regroup in the blink of an eye, and are quickly gone. I imagine the ball of fish bouncing across the ocean's floor.

It is with reluctance that I turn to the trail and start to climb. It's hard going. Standing upright is becoming increasingly challenging as I am having regular dizzy spells that are eroding my confidence. Hot rasps of breath escape from my overworked lungs. Energy levels are plummeting, along with my resolve. Finally at the top, I sit heavily and cradle my head in trembling hands. I fear this loss of energy and what the lack of food is doing to me. I am roused by a skink darting away from under me, having narrowly avoided being squashed. No doubt these rocky peaks are favoured sunbaking spots.

I stand and look to sea, raising a hand to shield my eyes from the glare. Gannets have joined the mix and are feeding. They drop like well-aimed stones into the steel grey water below. The continual squawking of ever hungry gulls – Kelp, Silver, and Pacific – fills the air, while around the rocky base of Pedra seals that are not fishing loll around, flippers in the air. Never have I seen such activity on the water.

I imagine myself as a bird, taking flight from the island and seeing all below me. Tipping my wing over Eddystone Rock, gliding first low, then higher towards the eastern horizon, I look for boats or a plane with a keen bird's eye. I circle in a wide northerly arc before turning south to navigate over Pedra's camel-like back. Dipping one way, then the other, I peer around humps to scour the sea south of the island. I am distracted by a large flock of Shearwaters flying in a south-westerly direction. I watch as, ever efficient in flight and thick in number, the birds appear to merge as one, resembling an enormous raft skimming across the surface of the ocean. It is an impressive sight. How I wish I could hitch a ride. In their wake, a gold-dusted sun shower creates a shimmering mist.

Eva appears, emerging from around the other side of the island. I can distinguish a dark band of damaged feathers where the wing was compromised. Despite the loss of some feathers, Eva's wing beat is sure and steady as she rises to my elevation. Her yellow-tipped beak comes close enough to hint at a kiss before turning, ocean waves providing lift as she deftly soars westward. I follow the bird's flight over the spread of the sea and into the approaching shower, which sidesteps, slow dancing towards the mainland coast line. Where the sun shower had played, Eva now appears, gliding on slow moving air currents above a boat, a boat being reeled in by Pedra.

smallest of the fishermen, surely little more than a boy, seems to be pleading my case. Our eyes meet and hold. Something is being dragged across the deck and with immense relief, I see it is a rubber dinghy. The lifeboat is being readied. Tears are streaming down my face as I continue to wave. The waves are sucking at me but I manage to hold myself upright.

It is the boy who clambers over the railing and drops neatly into the dinghy. With deft movements he manoeuvres the boat, watching as swell rides up the ledge and tugs at my legs, before turning his eyes directly to mine. As the boy nears, he gives me a thumbs-up. I give him a thumbs-up in turn and receive a grin of acknowledgment. In practiced hands, the dinghy rides fluidly atop the next wave as it speeds towards me. With acute concentration I focus on timing my leap for when the bow nudges the rocky shore, for the dinghy will ride in on a wave and just as quickly retreat. I don't hesitate as I leap, for this is my chance of rescue and I do not want the captain changing his mind. Landing safely in the dinghy, I look up to see the boy grinning beside me. My smile mirrors his; the happiest of smiles.

fifteen
# The fishing boat

A ladder snakes down over the mid-section of the fishing boat. It is an old steel boat, its bow sliding upwards, breaking the hard lines of the vessel. I see a small flag fluttering part way up the mast but neither a name nor number, which is unusual. These are the first close images I have of my rescue vessel. The faces looking down at me are anxious, smiles strained in an effort to welcome me. Yuto – who had introduced himself as I jumped in the dingy – is not only much practiced in dinghy handling, but has a calm and infectiously pleasing demeanour. It is thanks to Yuto's aptitude that I am quickly clambering up the ladder. I struggle at the railing. Roped forearms reach out to haul me aboard like a netted fish.

Collapsing at the feet of my rescuers, I weep tears of relief and have a strong impulse to kiss the deck. Preventing me from doing so is the assault to my senses. The stench is overpowering. I'm kneeling on slippery fish remains. A fish scale shines iridescent on the deck between my fingers. Blood and salt are deeply ingrained in the deck's surface. I hasten to my feet.

Regardless of shocked expressions, and momentarily forgetting about cultural differences – Yuto is Japanese, while the rest of the crew appear Indonesian in origin – I throw my arms around each fisherman in turn, thanking them joyfully. My body language is sure to be readily understood. My words may not be,

# UNDERTOW

as the men all speak at once in a language foreign to me. Palms together, I bow low in gratitude. This creates mirth and relaxes the atmosphere on deck. Yuto delightedly slaps the shoulder of the fisherman laughing beside him. Animated chatter is music to my ears after an absence of human interaction, despite not being able to understand what is being said.

Laughter dies quickly as an older man, weather-beaten and wearing a stern frown, appears on deck. He strides my way, stopping directly in front of me. I can feel the eyes of the crew appraising the situation. I look up at him and smile as broadly as I can. The man turns his back on me, throwing a brittle volley of words at the crew and jabbing at various pieces of equipment. His rough tone leaves little doubt that he expects to be obeyed. He is clearly the captain. The crew display a wary deference.

'Welcome aboard,' the captain says in English, finally giving me his full attention.

'Thank you,' I respond, my arms dropping lamely by my side as he steps away from me.

Although his mouth is smiling, his eyes are not, and I fear that the captain is displeased I am aboard his vessel. The crew go about their chores, heads lowered. With a frustrated air, the captain turns his attention to Yuto and waves his arm in the direction of the wheelhouse.

'Yuto, get this woman a blanket and hot drink, pronto.'

Yuto responds immediately. The rest of the men go about their business in silence, listening in, although I suspect that their understanding of the English language may not be as pronounced as Yuto's. The mood is dark. I have little time to ponder why, as I'm very happy to be aboard the vessel and there is so much to take in.

Yuto takes my arm and motions for me to follow him, briskly guiding a path past a hydraulic line hauler, drums, winches, and tubs of different sizes for lines and hooks, I guess. There is also a pile of buoys in the corner of the vessel. Notably absent are identification numbers on the buoys. Being familiar with fishing boats, I know all buoys are supposed to display the vessel identification number. An alarm bell rings in my head; the boat could be fishing illegally. It is a commercial fishing vessel that uses a long line with baited hooks at intervals to fish, a controversial fishing practice. It is much larger than *Mulwala*, around seventy to eighty feet in length. A working boat.

I observe little more of the details of the boat as I follow Yuto in a daze. My overloaded mind is becoming numb. Yuto leads me by the hand and encourages with carefully chosen words. Once down the companionway steps and in the main cabin, he gently motions for me to sit and hands me a glass of water. Thankful to be on the boat – regardless of why it is in Southern Tasmanian waters – tears slide down my cheeks, adding salt to the water I swallow greedily. I drink too fast and a coughing fit ensues. I collapse onto the cushioned seating.

Yuto pats my arm awkwardly, a crease between his brows. Lifting my head as the coughing subsides, I thank him for his care. Our conversation is stilted but Yuto's smile is full of warmth. How good it feels to be sitting on a seat and to have a caring soul beside me. The kettle whistles and Yuto stands to answer it. My head is spinning. My presence on the boat has created disquiet and the crew are obviously wary of the captain, but he did rescue me and for that I am eternally grateful. I am off Pedra Branca and on an operational boat. I am alive. I will, however, be relieved when I leave this boat; the tension is palpable and I'm not sure if I am the cause of it, or if it is a usual state of affairs. Hopefully, I will be back in Hobart by nightfall.

Fatigue threatens to overwhelm me. My body and mind scream for respite. Yuto produces a tray on which a teapot and cups balance beside a plate of biscuits. Shaped like little teddy bears, the biscuits and teapot are incongruous on a fishing boat. I reach for the biscuits as Yuto looks on indulgently.

The captain appears and sits stiffly to one side of me. He nods at Yuto to sit also and silence ensues while Yuto ceremoniously pours tea into three cups, serving first the captain, then me, and lastly himself. Biscuits are offered and the sweet, floury treats have my tastebuds on full alert. Yuto coaxes me to eat slowly as I reach for yet another biscuit. The captain watches on, quietly contemplating. I savour every biscuit, revelling in both the tea and the food. That I am on a Longline fishing boat sharing tea with a boat captain and kind cabin boy is as wondrous to me as surviving my leap onto Pedra Branca. An astrologer once told me I had a guardian angel on my shoulder watching over me. I now believe it. I momentarily let go of tension as I eat and drink.

Smiling, I introduce myself formally to the captain, holding out my hand to him and thanking him profusely. I only hope he will recognise my gratitude as sincere and not begrudge detouring from his fishing practices to rescue me. I am unsure if he has any idea who I am or that there is – most likely – an alert out for *Mulwala,* and for Sam and I. Taking my hand but briefly, the captain's eyes meet mine. He fails to introduce himself in turn.

'How and why were you on Pedra Branca, and alone?' he asks, scrutinising me.

I start to blurt out my story, tangling up words in my haste, telling him that Sam was on board the yacht with me, that he went overboard, and that the boat is now at the bottom of the sea.

I pause. Tears are streaming down my cheeks. My gut is clenched. I have to be vigilant until I reach home and need a moment to gather my thoughts.

'Captain, I'm starving. I mean no disrespect, but can I have something else to eat please?'

He barks out a command to Yuto in response.

Despite being a little guilty at the speed at which Yuto jumps up, I look directly at the captain and give him a brief outline of how I came to be on the island. I explain to him that my yacht had been close to Pedra when the storm hit and that she took on water; that I had little choice but to abandon my vessel, as I was sure *Mulwala* was going to succumb to the storm, either by sinking or running aground and shattering. He raises his eyebrows, his expression incredulous at my fortune to have scrambled onto Pedra Branca safely.

'I am incredibly lucky to have made it onto Pedra, and am truly grateful you have rescued me, captain. Have you heard an alert for the vessel *Mulwala* on your radio?'

The captain frowns with obvious consternation, the walnut creases of his face puckering as his woolly brows draw together. Yuto is rummaging about in the galley and I am momentarily distracted by enticing aromas.

'Can I use your radio please?' I ask the captain, becoming exasperated by his lack of responsiveness to me.

'Are you sure that your vessel has sunk?' he asks abruptly.

'I believe so. The weather took a turn for the worst – as you must know – and then *Mulwala*'s engine failed. We were close to rocks,' I add, choking back a sob of despair.

I'm speaking too fast, worried by the doubt written all over the captain's face. It seems he wants reassurance that *Mulwala* has sunk.

'The boat was taking on water quickly, captain. I am sure.'

He seems reassured by my answer and rubs a hand over his face as he nods. Moments pass as the captain mulls over my story. Suddenly standing, he thumps the table and yells something at Yuto I cannot understand. Yuto startles and drops a pot on the galley floor. It bangs loudly. The captain yells something else, then quickly disappears up the companionway steps.

'What's going on?' I ask, standing shakily.

Yuto refrains from answering me as he focuses on cleaning up the mess made on the galley floor. Approaching him, he stares at me blankly until I grab his arm imploringly.

'The captain does not want this,' he states with a worried frown.

'I have to use the radio, Yuto. Can you help me?' I plead, my hand still on his arm.

I search his gaze for comfort and reassurance, and while he looks at me kindly, I see no sign of the reassurance I seek.

Before I can say anything more, Yuto turns and dishes up a plate of steaming rice and fish, which he holds out to me. With his hand on one side of the plate, and mine on the other, we stare at each other. Surely, I am just overtired and all will be well. I was rescued after all, and now have food in front of me. The intentions of the captain cannot be bad; at least, I hope not.

'Please, eat,' Yuto says.

I sit and immediately stuff forkfuls of rice into my mouth. Yuto reaches out to me, offering me chopsticks as a trade for my eating utensils, wanting to slow my consumption of food. His warnings come too late as my stomach rebels against the sudden onslaught of food and I heave up my meal. Yuto has had the forethought to have an old pot in hand, and once more I am grateful to him. Wiping my mouth on the back of my hand, I apologise for the mess I have created.

'It's okay,' smiles Yuto, handing me a glass of water.

His compassion at least, is evident. Communication is so much more than words. Yuto gently wipes my face with a wet cloth, his ministrations rendering me lost for words.

Chewing slowly now with my eyes closed, I relish in the delicate flavours of the meal, even as my mind struggles to find answers. The sensation of a full stomach is blissful. Taking care to chew methodically, I try to make sense of the captain's strange reluctance to engage with me. I hope sustenance will help me to think clearly. Yuto brings me another pot of tea and patiently waits for me to eat and drink my fill. He is a caring young man – older than I had initially thought, perhaps in his mid-twenties – and reminds me of my son, Matt. Both have the ability to put others at ease. I swipe at my eyes, exhausted by emotion and trying to understand the situation.

'Yuto, do you have a pen and paper?' I ask.

He reaches for a pad and pencil and hands both to me. I write down my name, Sam's name, our yacht's name and number, and a rough account of incidents these past days, paying care to recall the limited details I know of Sam's disappearance.

'Yuto, has the captain alerted the mainland of my rescue?'

'No, Kay. No radio,' he replies sadly.

'Why not?' I ask, more loudly than I had intended.

'Kay, please eat and I will go and talk to captain, okay?'

'Okay, I will wait for a few minutes. But please tell him authorities will be

looking for me, and that this is urgent. Take this,' I add, handing him my notes.

Yuto agrees. He leaves the cabin with a reluctant air.

To believe anything other than we are on our way back to Hobart is too hard to contemplate. Regardless, it seems imperative that I get to the radio – it may not be available to crew, but all boats have a radio – to call authorities myself, however, I will adhere to Yuto's suggestion that he talk to the captain first. I look around but fail to see any sign of a radio below deck. I attempt to stand as I want to get up on deck and see what's going on, but as soon as I do so queasiness grips me again and I hastily sit, swallowing back vomit. Taking another sip of water, I wait for the sick feeling to subside. Yuto will be back in a minute.

*Sit tight, Kay. Trust.*

I cradle my head in my arms on the table in front of me and close my eyes, fatigue overwhelming me.

sixteen
# Thin air

It was in the nineties when the primal call of nature drew me to Nepal. School holidays meant my children could spend time with their cousins roaming around a large sheep property in Victoria's high country, giving me the opportunity to fulfil a childhood dream and go hiking in the Himalayas. When hiking, in the mountains most particularly, my mind and body are freed of stresses. I am intense by nature and physical activity calms me. I'm more in control. In contrast, inactivity can cause my thoughts to speed up and buzz uncomfortably. I end up feeling trapped and overwhelmed.

The timing felt right as I threw on my backpack and strode into Melbourne's Tullamarine airport to catch my flight to Kathmandu.

Tim Macartney-Snape wrote in his novel *Everest: from Sea to Summit*, 'Never has the miracle and beauty of life been as real and vivid as on a mountain top in clear weather; never has the feeling of the underlying union of all things and of being a part of it seemed so acute.'

Tim put into words what I have long felt in my heart.

Kathmandu in October 1994 was as I had imagined it to be, only bolder. It was vibrant, dusty, and intriguing. The city awakens the senses in a way befitting its status as the gateway to the highest mountain range on earth. At a heady elevation of 1,400 metres, there is a sharp sense of anticipation as hikers prepare for what is ahead. Walking from my hotel in search of a meal, I had to sidestep a shirtless man with a monkey on his shoulder. Prayer wheels spun and everywhere there was noise and activity. Sitting in the bowl-shaped valley of central Nepal, Kathmandu greets tourists brightly. I was fortunate to visit Nepal before political unrest and before the devastating 2015 earthquakes that rocked the nation, back when laughter, hope, and tourism flourished – as they will again.

As the Himalayan city enchanted, the mighty mountains enticed. I flew from Kathmandu to Lukla – the runway, at an altitude of 2,860 metres, is considered the most dangerous on Earth – in an old army helicopter that had seen better days. Wads of paper were stuffed in numerous holes, and it was impossible to speak above the shuddering, then roaring of the chopper once airborne. Regardless, it was a magical experience. Snow-covered mountains, impossibly high, reached up to touch the bluest of skies. The sight of the Himalayas from the air brought me to tears.

Lukla sits on the side of a sheer mountain in north-east Nepal, and it was from here that I started my trek to the summit of Kala Patthar, which sits at an altitude of 5,644 metres, above Everest Base Camp. As a child I had read about the first summiting of mighty Everest by Edmund Hilary and Tenzing Norgay over half a century ago, and had felt the mountains pull on me then. Not being a mountaineer, the summit of Everest was never a goal, however climbing to Kala Patthar – an excellent vantage point above Base Camp – to admire the mountains at close range certainly was.

It was not all pretty. In my Nepalese travel journal, I wrote of one day lying on a dirty blue tarpaulin – on which we ate our meals – and having an attack of the sillies, as Sasha, my daughter and I used to call our laughing fits. I wrote of the overflowing toilet close by, how it assaulted our senses; of the sherpa and cook blowing snot out of their noses like there was no tomorrow, and of nevertheless wanting to join the pair standing waist-deep in icy water, spitting and washing simultaneously. A good spit at altitude in the Himalayas helps the lungs to clear, needed after trekking dusty paths for weeks on end. I laughed until my sides ached and tears fell, rolling around on that blue tarpaulin, joyfully happy, exuberant, light and free. Such moments are rare in life.

I had tasted the essence of the Himalayan mountains, the air so pure it almost cracked on my tongue. I had stood atop a mighty peak and faced Everest reverently, oh-so-humbled to be where I was. With prayer flags fluttering atop Kala Patthar, a Golden Eagle had soared overhead, at home on a clear blue slate above the tallest mountains on the planet.

As the Dudh Koshi river flowed, so too did my thoughts tumble unhindered, uninhibited, onwards to a natural destination and conclusion. I danced to the light of the kitchen fire, music supplied by the beating of hands-on plastic jerry cans and on the bottoms of metal cooking bowls. I copied my Nepalese friends, mimicking birds and animals, not at all self-conscious in that environment.

Back home in Melbourne I had to make some tough decisions. Dad will say that I am running away when I outline my next adventure to him. The truth is, I choose to delve into new environments and experiences when overwhelmed, in order to come home with an open mind and a clear head. Dad likes to tackle things head on, or turn to work for clarity and focus. We just approached things differently, although with similar objectives, I believe. Life is too precious to put up with crap. I had learnt a lot since that first foray into the world of adventure with my colourful girlfriend.

The beauty of Nepal is in the essence, in the simplicity of just being. This experience would guide me in future years, back to the mountains and to environments where I could immerse myself in nature. I am then reminded of the beauty in moments. I can stop and be calm. When we pause to take a breath, we are better equipped to make decisions as to what to do next, or – as we cannot have control over everything – to accept when inaction is the best action. Sleep, like travel, gives us a fresh perspective.

seventeen
# The bay

A vibration under the seat rattles me awake. Chasing a memory, I recall dreaming of snow-covered mountains, a Golden Eagle, and the sensation of being as light as the high-altitude air. Languid, I seek to let sleep reclaim me and take me back to a peaceful place.

The present day weighs down on me, and it is with reluctance that I pull myself from slumber. Lying on a soft seat, cushion under my head and a blanket over me, the cloudiness of sleep beckons still. I lift my head with effort. The luxury of a blanket and pillow cannot be overstated. I will never underestimate comfort or take it for granted again. The world has many hard, jagged edges. Surely, I am entitled to savour this respite a little longer.

A gentle rolling sensation, distant voices, and the hum of an engine registers. I am on a fishing boat after being rescued from Pedra Branca. I am on my way back to Hobart. I push my protesting body into a sitting position and stretch. Home. The thought makes me smile.

Yuto, I presume, has thought to leave a glass of water on the table in front of me. I drink thirstily and, craving more water, look towards the galley. Pushing the blanket aside, I gingerly stand. All good. I make my way across the cabin with steady steps. It is a calm morning and the fishing boat is cutting the smooth water cleanly. Refilling my cup from the tap in the orderly galley, I pause to look out of the porthole above the sink. Confusion reigns as I see not the channel with the familiar outline of Bruny Island to one side and the rolling hills of the mainland on the other, but the high cliff faces of the South Coast. The fishing boat is not on route back to Hobart.

'What the hell is going on?' I exclaim, my reflection in the window revealing deep worry lines and general dishevelment.

Flummoxed, I try to think of reasonable explanations. Maybe the captain saw fish worthy of a detour, or the boat has been delayed due to mechanical concerns. Whatever the reason, I need to find out what's going on. Reaching for the tap, I hurriedly douse myself with water, swallowing thirsty mouthfuls as I splash my face. Running my fingers through my hair, I make my way across the cabin and reach for the companionway steps.

On deck all is quiet in the calm of a new day. The crew are working on the foredeck, backs bent attending to tasks at hand. The captain alone is at the helm in the wheelhouse.

The deck has been cleaned since last I stood on it. The fishing boat is fast approaching a remote bay on the South Coast. I had walked the South Coast Track with Sam in 2011. Sailing along this stretch of water en route to Port Davey in more recent times, I know the undulating lines and contours of Tasmania's southern coastline. The bay we are headed to is a long way from civilization.

I stare hard at the mainland but can make no sense of where we are and what we are doing. I can see no sign of recent or impending fishing activity – fishing gear is stowed – and if there is a problem with the boat, it is not evident. Why we are heading in the direction we are is a mystery. I have to get to a radio, immediately. A call to Tas Maritime on the VHF radio will answer the question as to whether authorities know of my whereabouts or not, and reassure me that Sam is in Hobart. I pray he is. Questions are mounting.

Troubled but trying not to show it, with what I hope is a friendly smile, I approach the wheelhouse. Heart hammering, I can only hope that answers are forthcoming. I slide open the door and address the man at the helm. 'Good morning, captain.'

He looks surprised to see me up and about, and in the wheelhouse. The tension in this confined space is palpable. That the captain does not want me here is blatantly obvious, as his stare is lethal. However, he rearranges his face and returns my greeting.

'Hello, Kay, good to see you are feeling better. Did you sleep well?'

Two can play at this game of pretence.

'I slept well and am feeling much better, thank you.' The radio is situated behind the seat on which the captain sits. I start to edge towards it. 'Nice boat you have here.'

The captain grunts. His focus is directed to the fast-approaching shoreline.

Acting on instinct, I make a lunge for the radio, grab it, and press in the talk button.

'Tas Maritime, this is Kay from the vessel *Mulwala*. Does anyone …?'

The captain springs from his seat. 'What the hell are you doing, woman?! Get out of my wheelhouse, now!' Spittle rains over me as he snatches the radio from my hands.

'Please, tell me what's going on,' I ask, determined not to be undermined by this man. 'I give you my word I will not cause any trouble for you on my return to Hobart,' I add, facing him squarely.

'Out,' he yells, pushing me aside and jabbing his finger towards the door to emphasise his order.

I stand firm. 'Have you even notified anyone that I'm alive?'

'I've helped you all I can. You'll be dropped off in the bay ahead,' he states, gesticulating towards the shore.

'But why? You have a responsibility to take me back to Hobart.'

He bellows over my head in response and Yuto appears, hurriedly pulling me with him back across the deck. It makes no sense.

'What's going on, Yuto?'

Motioning me back below deck, Yuto promises to explain what is happening if I just cooperate. I trust him and, although unwilling to go back below deck, I am desperate for answers. I vehemently hope that another fishing vessel has heard the conversation in the wheelhouse when I momentarily had possession of the VHF radio. The local coastal patrol will hear if it was on channel sixteen, the international emergency station – but was it? I had failed to check.

This is crazy. This isn't supposed to be happening. I was rescued. I am on a boat.

*Why the hell am I not on my way back to Hobart?*

Yuto motions me to sit on the seat I recently vacated. He bustles about making tea and pushing items into what was already a full grab bag. I'm immobilised by shock. I register Yuto putting tea before me and telling me to drink.

He pauses, staring intently at me. 'Kay, the captain, he needs fish.'

'What do you mean? He has a quota to fill?'

'No questions. Please get things you need before it's too late,' Yuto pleads, gesturing towards the galley.

'Am I in danger?' I ask in alarm.

Yuto is stuffing more items into the bag; a camping stove, matches, and a first aid kit. He opens cupboards in the galley and gestures for me to help myself. I quickly put the items he tosses my way into a bag. He assures me that the fishing boat has previously sought shelter in the bay ahead and that there is a plentiful fresh water supply.

'Is there a boat coming for me?' I ask, desperately hoping that the answer will be yes.

Yuto looks scared. 'No, Kay. Maybe another boat come. Not this boat. I do not know.'

*Shit.* I hunch my shoulders in despair.

The captain's voice hurtles down the companionway steps. 'Yuto, take Kay to shore in the dinghy now!'

I see a sleeping bag through the open doorway of a cabin. 'Do you have a spare sleeping bag, Yuto?'

'Take it, and hurry please,' he replies.

In minutes I have two additional bags in my hands, along with my grab bag, and am being pulled up on deck by Yuto. His insistence that we will both suffer if we do not move pronto injects life into my legs.

The captain is storming across the deck towards us. Yuto is already launching the dinghy. There is a rousing cry from the rest of the crew, and I gasp as I see them lunging at each other and tumbling over the deck, shouting and throwing their fists about. The captain heaves one of the men off another and in doing so cops a kick to his head. Stunned, he reels, bellowing.

I jump into the waiting dinghy. It now seems safer to be off the fishing boat.

'Go, Yuto!' I shout uselessly, as we are already moving away from the fishing boat. I fall back onto a seat.

'Sorry, Kay, sorry,' Yuto says repeatedly as the dinghy speeds towards the beach.

I sit in stunned silence, watching as the fishing boat retreats in the distance and we move along rapidly. In no time at all we are almost on the beach.

'Radio for help; do that for me please, Yuto. You have the paper I gave you – it has all the information authorities need.'

He acknowledges me with a sad smile, working the tiller, eyes focused on the shore.

'Will you be okay? Will the rest of the crew be alright?'

He nods. I don't feel particularly reassured but tell myself that the captain needs crew.

The small boat touches the shoreline just as the morning sun finds the beach. Yuto hurriedly helps me off the dinghy with my possessions and additional supplies. He thrusts the sleeping bag at me. It is all happening so fast. I try one last time.

'Please call the authorities for me, Yuto. Tell them where I am, that *Mulwala* has sunk. Tell Sam I'm okay.'

He leans towards me, giving me a quick hug. I hug him in turn, salty tears wetting his t-shirt. Yuto has been integral in saving my life and I do not want to let him go. Nor do I want to be alone again.

'Thank you, Yuto,' is all I can manage.

'Okay, all okay,' he replies simply, stepping away from me. He looks so young and unsure of himself in that instant that I know I can ask no more of him.

Emotionally spent, I stand back. The fishing boat is idling offshore and I see the captain standing impatiently on deck, beckoning to Yuto and shouting something I cannot make out. The crew have retreated to different ends of the vessel.

Yuto gives me a small smile, bows, and leaps into the dinghy. He fires up the outboard and is quickly gone.

Dumping my supplies on the sand, I put my hands on my knees and watch forlornly as the dinghy arrives at the fishing boat. Wash races towards me, retreating just short of my toes. I hold onto Yuto's smile as the boat becomes but a smudge on the horizon.

# UNDERTOW

I cross the sand and turn my back on the sea, stopping to allow the quiet to settle around me.

Breathe, Kay, breathe.

Minutes pass. I sniff. There it is again, a sweet aroma. I swivel around, looking for the source of the scent. The stench of bird shit and kelp that had pervaded on Pedra Branca is absent, so too the aroma of fish flesh and guts that was familiar on the fishing boat, as it is on all fishing boats. I have sorely missed the smells of the Tasmanian bush. Eucalyptus lingers in my nostrils and another smell, sharper, infiltrates as I turn my head.

The feeling of sand beneath my feet and sunshine on my body – warmth enveloping me as surely as Yuto's smile had – is soothing. Birdsong dances through the nearby trees. I reach my arms up high and wide and embrace the smells and sounds of coastal bush. I am back on Tasmanian soil (well, sand, but it is Terra firma). The life-threatening events of the past days are behind me. I am alive. What lies ahead, I will deal with. I'm not going to give up now.

There it is again, the other scent I am detecting. It is not my imagination; at the edge of sea and bush, a small puff of wind carries the distinctive aroma of marijuana towards me. Looking above the uneven line of scrub in front of me, I detect a faint, whispery line of smoke. My immediate thought is that hikers who have carried dope in with them are camping close by. I am not alone!

'Hello, anyone there?' I call out in greeting, my voice startling in the calm bay.

The whisper of the trees answers me.

I walk up the beach, through scraggly Acacia and scattered gums to a small clearing. There in front of me is a weather-worn man, long-haired and very lean. I am drawn to the lines and contours of the man's face. His gaze is intense as he appraises me from under greying brows. He has a broodiness about him, and his posture is that of a weary traveller. He does not look threatening, unlike the boat captain. Deep tiredness is etched on his face and evident in the downturned corners of his mouth. A fat joint droops from his lips. With calm deliberation, the stranger takes the joint from his mouth to trail it in long fingers.

Showing nicotine-stained teeth, he grins in greeting, and in doing so his appearance is transformed. 'Coffee?'

Just like that. If my sudden appearance has surprised him, he hides it well.

'Coffee?! Ah, yes please,' I respond, somewhat disbelievingly. 'Do you have a satellite phone, or an EPIRB?'

He shakes his head. My shoulders drop and I sigh in frustration.

He pats the fallen tree branch he is using as a seat, beckoning for me to sit. 'I don't bite,' he states amicably.

My instincts tell me that he means no harm, and so I dump my belongings and sit. There is a peacefulness about the stranger, despite his haggard appearance. Having obviously intruded on this man's solitary time, I sip my coffee and let the air settle around us, collecting my own thoughts. Weird is becoming the norm.

It's good to hear the sounds of the bush, birds and insects, and the swish and wash of water on a gentle shoreline.

'Aaron,' he says by way of introduction.

'Kay.'

'Knew I'd see someone. Heard the boat.' Aaron speaks conversationally and I am comfortable in his presence, despite the oddity of our situation. 'So, what brings you here then?' he asks. His direct gaze draws me in, interested and inviting trust.

That's all the opening I need. Aaron listens intently as I tell him of my harrowing ordeal, starting with setting off on *Mulwala* from Hobart. He raises his eyebrows when I mention Pedra Branca and smiles broadly when I relay my time with the Shy Albatross and tell him how Eva directed my eyes to the fishing boat. Aaron does not show doubt as I tell my story, merely curiosity and intrigue. After outlining more recent events that led me to this beach, Aaron and I discuss the fishing boat.

'Fishing illegally by the sounds of it. They would have been happy to see the last of you, I reckon,' he states matter-of-factly.

'Yep, that was my conclusion as well.'

'Bloody arsehole; that captain.'

I shrug. 'Maybe I'm lucky he picked me up at all.'

Aaron mulls over my story, all the while puffing away. His eyes travel to the belongings I dropped beside the log. 'Any tobacco in those bags?'

I throw back my head and laugh, the sound startling Aaron and myself in turn and triggering raucous bird cries in response.

eighteen
# Turua Beach

I empty the contents of my bags on the ground, keen to see what additions have been made. My supplies have been well fortified thanks to the generosity of Yuto. I am both grateful and puzzled in equal measure. Aaron looks on. If he is disappointed that I have no tobacco, he hides it well.

A small camping stove, fuel, lighter, a battered but serviceable aluminium pot, fork, and first aid supplies have been placed in a separate bag. There is also a package, heavily wrapped in foil and reeking of fish. The old sleeping bag is of good quality and promises warmth. It must have provided another with warmth and comfort many times over. A wave of guilt washes over me with the realisation that I left the crew one sleeping bag short.

Yuto has wedged a packet of black tea and sugar in a tin mug for me, and seeing the thoughtfulness of this gift nearly brings me to tears again. Knowing my supplies are more than adequate for a few nights in wilderness is reassuring, however, my hope is that rescuers are at this very minute looking for me.

'Have you seen any other boats recently?'

'Nah, not with the weather as it has been,' Aaron replies.

'Any sign of the Westpac chopper?'

'Not since some young fella broke his ankle in an attempt to kayak from Recherche Bay around to Port Davey a few weeks ago. From the mainland he was, didn't know this stretch of coastline. Not a clue about the weather in these parts. Bloody lucky he made it to shore at all.'

'That was brave of him,' I reply, stunned that anyone would attempt such a feat.

I repack my supplies as I ponder my new situation. 'What about hikers then; anyone likely to have a phone or radio?'

'Nah.' Aaron studies my expression. 'I usually see someone at least a couple of times a week in these parts and reckon on some passers-by soon.'

'I hope so,' I respond, wanting reassurance. At least I have company and I'm safe, for the time being. I just have to be patient a little longer.

Aaron is as delighted as I am of my newfound treasures. 'All set for a comfortable stay at Turua Beach then.'

'I won't be staying long.'

Aaron merely shrugs. He is seemingly spent from conversation. I sit beside him, at ease and happy to think my own thoughts.

Yuto had dropped me off at what I now realise is Little Deadmans Bay. Rounding a rocky outcrop, I had followed the trail of smoke from Aaron's cigarette onto Turua Beach, prettier and less rock-strewn than the adjoining bay. I remember the area from my hike with Sam. I look around. Yes, this is the picturesque campsite Sam and I had said we would come back to one day. It is set behind low dunes with sparse vegetation. Here there is shelter, the sand is soft and the artistic, nature-inspired decorations of trekkers provides a surprising and welcoming rest spot.

The fish needs to be cooked, and I'm suddenly ravenous. Asking Aaron if he has a frying pan, he jumps up to rummage at the back of his tent. Taking the coffee pot off his Trangia, he sets the frying pan on the camping stove. Aaron's equipment must take a bit of hauling. Looking more intently at my companion, I note the loose pants and belt pulled tight, hollow cheeks and sallow skin. I am curious to hear his story in turn. He is not a picture of good health and yet here he is, in this remote region, welcoming me to this campground with friendly overtures.

The day had opened like an unexpected letter, startling me with plans altered and a new course set. Sitting with Aaron at Turua Beach, I feel a sense of familiarity and comfort. After hiking and camping all of my adult life, the simple routines required of camp life bring me calm. My mind and body are desperate for a break, for a sense of normality, for a period of rest, uncomplicated and easy.

As fish sizzles in the pan, birdsong rises higher, following the sun, and waves lick the shore. Aaron is focused on his self-appointed cooking task and disinclined to talk. We eat in companionable silence. Once we have satisfied our hunger, Aaron rolls a joint, taking his time as he does with all of his movements. Hesitating but a moment – the last time I smoked marijuana was many years ago – we pass the joint back and forth between us. The smoke – and the coffee, which is strong and bitter – scours my throat.

Aaron startles me from my reveries. 'I guess you want to know how I ended up here.' He looks at me frankly.

'Sure, but only if you want to tell me.'

He squats on the ground before me, picking up a stick and absently scratching patterns in the sand. He lets the minutes pass by, lost in his own thoughts, the furrow between his brows deepening. As he starts talking, he puts down the stick and rests his forearms on lean thighs. His tale is an age-old love story about a man who falls in love with a younger woman, then has his heart broken when she outgrows the relationship. Aaron's lover had initially embraced him and his lifestyle, and soon after meeting they had moved into a house together. They spent their days outside of work hiking and rock climbing.

'Happiest I've ever been,' says Aaron, scuffing the toe of his boots in the sand. 'She got more self-indulgent as time went on. Said she was bored, dismissing me and my ideas, doing her own thing, leaving little time for us.'

Finally, she rejected him outright, packed her bags and left.

'Didn't know what to do, couldn't think right,' he says.

As I listened to Aaron, I realised he was unable to come to terms with the relationship breakdown, succumbing to depression. Eventually anger took hold of him and, struggling to get beyond a negative state, Aaron chose to go walkabout. Since that time, he has been walking in remote regions of Southern Tasmania, setting up camp at locations he takes a fancy to, sometimes for weeks at a time. Astounded, I ask about food supplies.

'Friends,' he responds. 'I'm lucky, I have good friends who care for me, who understand.'

His friends have rallied to support him in a time of need. Small groups hike into wilderness areas to drop off food, supplies and sometimes mail. The drops have been organised well in advance. Occasionally they give Aaron a brief respite from his self-imposed solitude by meeting him at a pre-determined spot, although paths seldom cross. Aaron moves at his own pace. He tells me he has a couple of adult children back home.

'When is the next drop, and where? Is it here? Do they carry radios?' I ask excitedly.

'A mate just left me a few days back, Kay. Won't be another till next month.'

I want to scream in frustration. 'What about your kids, though? How do you contact them?'

'I don't,' he replies simply. 'Friends and my kids help give me a reason to keep going, but that doesn't mean we talk much.'

Aaron is unlike anyone I have ever met. I'm baffled by this man but am getting used to the way he speaks, keeping words to a minimum. He looks a little sheepish now, almost as if he has revealed too much. After a pause, he goes on.

'Sometimes the animals get to the food before me. Mostly the packages survive as they're left in tin boxes. Yep, good when I get them. A bit like Christmas.' He chuckles.

As Aaron speaks, I fill in the gaps. He talks passionately about trying to preserve Tasmania's south-west wilderness. It seems this man has been a tireless wilderness campaigner for a large part of his adult life. He knows this region well. He has been in the Southern Tasmanian wilderness for three months to date, time a slow healer.

Dumbfounded by Aaron's story, I can only shake my head in wonder. This land is raw, primitive, and while being beautiful, poses great challenges. I can't wait to get home, and yet here is someone who has chosen to basically go it alone and to live for months in rugged wilderness. To have the ability to survive in this country, solo and for an extended period, takes a special type of person. I'd go crazy – spending months, rather than a few days or weeks hiking in wilderness, is a vastly different ball game to going on a weekend hike.

'If ever I plan to spend long out here, I know where to get some good tips,' I say, smiling at my new friend. For the first time since I woke up on *Mulwala*, when confusion and fear reigned, my muscles are no longer bunched up.

The sun has moved across the sky and I'm pleasantly relaxed from food, conversation, and marijuana. I prop myself up on the log. In this state it is easier to trust that help is on its way. However, a rescue plane or boat needs a marker of some sort to indicate my location.

'I need to make some sort of signal,' I mumble, hauling myself upright. My body is screaming for sleep. Aaron is quick to dissuade me from making a signal fire on the beach.

'Too much effort and no boats or planes at this time of day. Morning would be best,' he reasons.

Determined to ensure my position is marked, I retrieve the high-vis sheet from my belongings. I struggle with laying out the sheet, which threatens to escape in a puff of wind. Seeing my efforts, Aaron steps in to help me, albeit reluctantly; after the dope and food, we could both do with sleep. We spread out the neon sheet and secure it on the sand with stones we find on the rocky headland between Turua Beach and Little Deadmans Bay. Our efforts may not create the neatest results but we work together easily and soon have the high-vis sheet displayed to advantage.

We head slowly back up the beach to our sheltered campsite, lost in our own individual thoughts. The pleasure of being on land again is palpable. Mental images of when I had hiked the South Coast Track with Sam weave in shades of light and colour. It was a mega hike, an eighty-five-kilometre journey from Melaleuca in the south-west of the state to Cockle Creek in the bottom most corner of south-east Tasmania. By my calculations it would be roughly a three-day walk to Cockle Creek and civilisation from my current position. To go in a westerly direction to reach Melaleuca, where there is a small runway, would require a longer and more arduous journey, the formidable Iron Bound Ranges to be crossed.

*It won't come to that.*

*Why then,* I wonder, *am I doing the calculations?*

Dad would be pleased I have a practical back-up plan. I smile, thinking how good it will be to see him and Mum again.

I amble around the campsite, exploring and pondering where best to unroll my sleeping bag. I can't fight sleep much longer. Aaron has drifted down to the beach. On my own, I take in all around me. Turua Beach entices trekkers to linger. It is not just the sheltered campsite, but the made-for-the-movies beach setting that appeals. Oh, and the fact that it is very remote. Tucked in behind the dunes, Turua Beach is the reward for those who make it here. Wind chimes created from shells strung on fishing wire, driftwood, and flotsam adorn the campsite.

Making some order of my belongings and respecting Aaron's space, I fashion a camping area for myself at the edge of the clearing. I'm close to the dunes and can hear the ocean and, hopefully, anything that passes this way. Unrolling the sleeping bag, I throw off my outer layers of clothing and cocoon myself in warm down. My eyelids flutter and the breeze carries my sleeping breath over the dunes and across the sea.

Dream sounds; squeak and pull of sheets, boat lines strained. I am back aboard *Mulwala*, waking to a different day. Boiling the kettle, I make two mugs of tea and take them up on deck. Handing a mug to Sam, I am vaguely aware that he has an opaque form, the outline of his body clear but the middle not filled in.

'The helm is not cooperative, honey,' he grumbles. He demonstrates, turning the wheel first one way and then the other so that I see the resistance. *Mulwala* is locked on a course.

'What is, simply is,' I declare. I pat the seat beside me, and with an exasperated sigh Sam sits at my side. We sip our tea.

'What will we do?' he muses as much to himself as to me, shoulders slumped, un-Sam like.

I put my hand on his arm in a gesture of reassurance. It is normally Sam reassuring me; he is the practical one. 'The Shy

Albatross will pull us along. See how he drags the boat through the water?'

Rope in beak, coming from a bridle at *Mulwala*'s bow, the albatross starts to pull our vessel, strong and sure.

Sam looks forward and nods. 'So be it. We won't know where we are going, though.' As an afterthought he adds, 'That'll suit you, honey.'

I raise my eyebrows and our eyes meet over the steaming mugs of tea. Taking my hand, Sam smiles and, with a flap of its wings, the albatross draws *Mulwala* from the sea, bow pointed skywards. Water streams down the sides of the yacht, creating a waterfall to the Southern Ocean, bejewelled in the dancing light.

I laugh delightedly. Sam pulls me close, our laughter rolling down the waterfall and bouncing over gentle waves.

nineteen

# Aaron

I wake to see pinpricks of light shimmering on a black palette above me. The night sky is vast. There is no sound of a waterfall, only a gentle lapping where the inquisitive sea meets shoreline. Lying still, my ears become attuned to night sounds and I breathe deeply to regain my sense of time and place. Smoke lingers in the sheltered campground. I follow the scent of tobacco until my eyes rest on a red glow. In the darkness I make out Aaron squatting, limbs bent at sharp angles. I sense he is at ease, drawing regularly on his cigarette while night wraps around us.

Closer to me, a scampering indicates that bush critters are exploring under cover of darkness. Wombats, spotted-tail quolls, bush rats and mice, pademelons, and possums inhabit these coastal shores. I recall camping close by with Sam, our tent enduring the onslaught of tiny teeth – belonging to bush rats, we suspected – scavenging for food.

Aaron is motionless, his dark outline blending in with the environment. He is a quiet, contemplative man. After months in the bush, the sound of night creatures foraging for food scraps at campsites is no doubt commonplace to him. Aaron will be familiar with the abundant wildlife in this area, and will undoubtedly, routinely, store any food safely before nightfall. Sam and I learnt to do that the hard way, for although we stored food in our tent, we did not bag it. Bush rats considered it fair game.

Rustling overhead catches my attention. It is an exploratory possum. Beneath an impossibly brilliant starlit sky, the branches of tea tree and banksia fan gently as a breeze whispers past. I stretch long in my sleeping bag, toes nudging the bottom of my warm cocoon. A pebble or stick protrudes underneath my leg and I shift slightly to avoid it.

Aaron turns his head as I move, the whites of his eyes visible. His cigarette glows as he inhales. Finding the bulk of my supine body silhouetted in the darkness, he nods then turns away to resume his night vigil. Snug and warm, I am content to lie a little longer; the respite from movement, action, and worry is alluring.

Aaron had briefly recounted events that had led him on his journey here, however, there is much more I do not know. He is an unusual man, seemingly without threat, malice, or expectations. He is somewhat of an enigma to me. While pleased to have someone to talk to, he has also made it clear that he wants to be left in peace.

'I need rescue about as much as a hole in the head,' he told me. 'Good to have companionship for a day or two just the same,' he added, seeing my look of surprise.

Our shared meal of fish was welcomed, though if I had arrived at this campsite with nothing, I sense that Aaron would be a generous host regardless. He is interesting company, listens intently and misses little, with non-judgmental appraisal. In normal, everyday life, it takes us a while to trust someone. Trust is generally something that is earned. In adverse situations, we have to make decisions more quickly. I will simply have to trust my instincts. I like Aaron and am glad I have found a friend.

Nudging my foot, a wombat that has wandered into camp gets a rude shock as I kick it reflexively. Sitting upright, my eyes now accustomed to the darkness, I see Aaron lean over the coffee pot. He unfolds his body and walks towards me, settling a steaming mug of the caffeine rich brew beside me.

'Thank you, what service,' I say in appreciation, picking up the battered mug.

Aaron nods, the hint of a smile on his lips. He goes back to squatting by his stove as I wriggle out of the sleeping bag and move to be by his side. He is cooking up a stew of some kind and my stomach growls with pleasure. As he carefully stirs the stew, Aaron informs me that he has decided to move on the next day. 'It's time I headed bush again.'

'No,' I cry in dismay. 'I have just found a friend. Surely, we can help each other. I trust you. You can trust me.'

Aaron raises his eyebrows as he dishes stew into bowls. He offers no response to my outburst. I shrug and open my mouth to ask him why he wants to part ways so quickly, but I am distracted by the meal he has placed in my hands.

The stew is delicious, wholesome and aromatic. Savouring the moment and the company, which may be short-lived, I try not to be freaked out by the possibility of being alone again. Surely, I can convince Aaron I will not be in his way; that together we can do better.

While his desire for solitude is evident, it seems clear to me that Aaron is unwell and I fear his isolation will only exacerbate any issues he has. However, I have no right to question his intentions. Aaron is entitled to make his own choices, as we all are.

Instead, I ask, 'What's in this stew? It's delicious.'

'Wallaby,' my companion informs me, 'flavoured with bush herbs, onions and potatoes.'

The only meat I eat back home is fish. I wouldn't think of eating wallaby in regular circumstances; however, my tastebuds are buzzing and I'm loving this meal.

'Do you eat wallaby regularly?' I ask.

'Yep, bush tucker is a necessity out here.'

I nod. If we are going to survive in harsh environments, we need to work with what we have and what is on offer. As coffee is poured – from an endless coffee pot, it seems – stories flow freely. I hope to build further trust over conversation, praying Aaron will change his mind and we can stick together for a bit. My gut is telling me Aaron needs a friend as much as I do.

We have more than one thing in common. Aaron too has lived on a boat in a marina in Hobart. Although coincidental, the fact that Aaron has done so immediately resonates. Only a small percentage of Tasmanians actually live on boats, although many in this state own fishing or pleasure boats. I have met some interesting characters at Kings Pier Marina and have learnt over time that, although the marina has its own community, people who live aboard vessels generally appreciate their privacy to be respected. Some stay but a short while when in transition, others for years.

'For Sam and me it's convenient, as we both live and work on the water. Boating communities are pretty cool, and tight,' I add.

'I like to be able to pack up when the mood takes me, when people get too much,' he responds.

A quietness envelops the campground. I could just put on my shoes in the morning and start walking. Now that I have had a bit of rest and food, it might be possible. When I get to an open beach my attempts to signal for help will be enhanced. Prion Beach stretches for around five kilometres and is the perfect area to make a big signal fire on. It's not too far away. If Sam has been rescued, or has found his way back to Hobart by other means, he'll be worried sick about me. If that is the case, though, surely, I would have seen a rescue helicopter out searching for me before now – unless searchers are focusing on Bruny Island and inland water ways. But what if Sam is not back in Hobart?

*Stop it, Kay. These questions won't get you anywhere. Just start walking.*

My coffee has gone cold and my head is spinning from caffeine, smoking, and thoughts that tumble around like pebbles tossed in the sea. Losing myself in Aaron's stories lessens the weight of my predicament. Both of us share a love of hiking. We chat about Hobart, of kunanyi/Mount Wellington and how its dark outline is formidable as it looms protectively over the city and waterways. From the Ice House track, a favourite walk of mine and Sam's on the mountain, the view over Southern Tasmania is resplendent on a clear day. The ridge part of this track overlooks the Southern Mountain ranges, which Aaron speaks about with passion. I tell him about one winter day when I walked the Ice House track and it was encrusted in thick ice, creating a window to clear water that rushed underneath as melt occurred. Feeling like Alice peering through the looking glass, I had watched the flow of water under my feet as it moved swiftly over pebbles and caused plants to arch over, succumbing to the stream's rush.

'I've seen similar in the mountains,' Aaron comments. 'The ice and snow might make for cold conditions, but when weather sets in you can be sure of rewards at some stage.'

Night closes protectively around us as Aaron and I share another joint and tell stories.

The Western Arthur Range is considered one of the most remote, wild, and challenging hiking areas in Australia. Aaron informs me it was here where he found the prints of a large animal that he was unable to identify. He did a bit of research and was amazed at how closely the prints appeared to resemble those of the extinct Thylacine, otherwise known as the Tasmanian tiger. Some believe the Thylacine still exists and if it does, the wilderness of south-west Tasmania is where it will be, hiding from man who hunted the species and valued its striped pelt more than the animal itself.

As the stars crowd the sky, Aaron talks about the rivers he has kayaked down and his love of the Franklin in particular. Aaron was a long-term campaigner to protect this river from damming. What a victory for that mighty river.

Night sounds become amplified as the lengths of silence in our conversation extend. I look around me as the moon reaches height and illuminates the campground.

'Hey, Aaron? Can we please stick together a bit longer? I could do with the help of an expert bushman, and I'd like to help you in turn.'

'What? I don't need any help. Thanks anyway, Kay.'

Aaron turns away from me and starts to wrap up food items. I star. at his back and wonder at his words.

'I don't know if I can do the row across the lagoon on my own, Aaron.'

He glares at me, then sighs in resignation.

I am drunk on the weight of a star-studded heaven, caffeine and weed giving clarity to each pinprick of light. Branches overhead sway rhythmically and wombats forage, their squat bodies pushing with intent around camp debris. A possum ring-tails it up the tree branch behind us. His round eyes stare at me boldly as he pauses in his exploration, scampering when I move. My head tilts forward, eyelids heavy once more.

I drag myself into wakefulness before the birds have begun their morning calls. My neck is sore, despite my head being cushioned by a jacket. I feel my hip keenly where it is pressed against the log I'm lying on. It's still bruised from when I hauled myself onto Pedra.

I push myself into a sitting position and hear a gentle snoring from Aaron's tent. Aaron's gestures of kindness, such as placing his jacket placed under my head, add to my fuddle-headedness; that and the after-effects of weed. Aaron had consented to walking together for the day but didn't appear too happy about it.

I'm suffering for the long night. My head thumps. Cold and disorientated, I slip my arms into the jacket, wrapping it around me as I emerge from the shadowed campground and walk out onto the beach. Blood returns to my extremities as I pace the sand, disjointed thoughts bouncing around as I attempt to clarify my plans.

A sea eagle dips low, small crabs circle into hastily made sand retreats, and an immature school of fish – white bait – hightail it from the shallows into the deeper water of the bay. The sun's rays have not yet reached the beach and I pull the collar of my coat up higher. A stiff morning breeze snaps at the ocean, and out beyond Turua Beach I can see white caps on the waves.

Aaron has agreed to strike out along the coast and accompany me as far as New River Lagoon, at which point he will turn inland. Guidebooks clearly stipulate hikers respect fellow trekkers and that a boat is left at either side of the lagoon. Aaron offered to row me across the lagoon, then return the boat to the opposite shore, dragging the second dinghy behind. He would then return to join me on the eastern shore, ensuring dinghies are on either side of the lagoon. I had readily agreed to his offer. There is no other way across the lagoon than to row, and I remember Sam and I having fun with the dinghies when we had reached New River Lagoon. It is true that for some reason I am unable to row in a direct line, and Sam cracks up when I attempt to do so.

One misfortune after another has thwarted my efforts to find Sam and to get safely back to Hobart and yet, albeit at a snail's pace, I am getting closer to home. After the storm, I had been so sure rescue would come. If a search party was trying to find me, they had yet to succeed. By continuing to walk along the coast, I have a good chance of being spotted by a plane or boat scouring the coastline, and plan on making signal fires where I can to aid that process. It's good to know I will be walking in the right direction, to safety, to Cockle Creek; to civilization. There I would find a ranger's station and home would then be less than a half day drive away on a sealed road. Not allowing my thoughts to focus on any other scenario but Sam having reached land and commencing a search for me, I trust my heart to guide me. I'm keen to set out as early as possible, despite a sore head. Maybe we will be seen on Prion Beach as we make our way to the lagoon.

I hustle back to the campground and set about making coffee for Aaron and me. The sooner I can rouse Aaron, the quicker we can farewell Turua Beach.

twenty
# Finding purchase

The damp forest drips and muffles sound as I push through the undergrowth. Carrying both Aaron's and my water bottles, I step over a fallen tree branch, one leg straddling the slick branch. I slip as I try to find purchase and promptly land on my backside. With water bottles strewn, the dank smell of rotting vegetation is thick in my nostrils. Crossly, I push myself into a sitting position. My clothes are slimy and the rich earth and moss that form a cushioned forest floor are now smeared across my rear end. Checking the water bottle lids are securely fastened, it is a relief to see I have not spilled any of the water that I have so carefully collected.

Boat shoes do not have the heavier tread desired for hiking. Careful negotiation will be required on the hike across slippery forest trails, winding up and over Menzies Bluff, before the descent to the beach. Prion Beach is a long stretch of sandy beach before New River Lagoon. I am both nervous to leave and excited to get going, in equal measure. How precarious one's security becomes when life is nearly lost; my attachment to this campground surprises me. However, I will not reach home or find Sam sitting here any longer. My strength and energy reserves are replenished enough to get moving. It's time to act.

Our camp is dismantled; I take one final look around me. A slight breeze plays in the trees and the shell mobiles chime in farewell. A poem that has been etched into a broad, flat rock at the campground entrance is barely discernible, wind and weather having sanded words away. Retrieving a knife from my belongings, I squat down beside a similar rock that is close by. It is smooth and shaped a bit like Tasmania. I pause as I string words together in my mind, and then I'm making sharp scratches on the rock, etching out a poem. I send the singer Bobby Darin a silent thank you for his song *Beyond the Sea* which gives me inspiration.

> *Beyond the sea*
> *my heart did soar*
> *seeing this stretch of pretty shore*
> *never again a sailboat shall be*
> *lost to the sea*
> *and to me*
> *cast on this beach*
> *I was forlorn*
> *until Turua Beach welcomed me*
> *Beyond the sea*
> *my heart did soar*
> *seeing this stretch of pretty shore.*

As the rough poem takes shape, I think about Bobby's lyrics, and my belief that I will see Sam again beyond the sea and back on Terra firma.

I wonder if my poem will ever be read by another. No matter; I write because it feels good to do so, and I need to somehow express my gratitude for Turua Beach. I am thankful for this healing place that is safe and welcoming, and for Aaron, who I met here. I see Aaron waiting for me and hastily roll the rock back where I had found it. Turning away from Turua Beach, I follow my companion out of the campground.

Aaron and I have fashioned a sling of sorts from a silk sleeping bag liner given to him by a friend in which to carry my possessions. It looks a bit like a fat sausage, flung over one shoulder across my back, the far end of the sheet pulled under my other arm and the sheet ends tied at my chest. The sling is an efficient way of carrying my gear and it's great to have my hands free.

Aaron declared he had failed to sleep in the silk sheet once, the concept strange after a lifetime of sliding directly into a sleeping bag. He told me of his fondness for his first sleeping bag, the one he had bought for the Franklin River blockade.

'It had a fleecy tartan lining although the bag was heavy and lumpy. I slept like a baby in that thing,' he adds with a faraway look in his eyes.

I smile in response, glad that Aaron is chatty today and happy to have his company. I so enjoy listening to Aaron's stories, as they all seem to resonate with me. Picking up a sturdy stick, I hop across a small creek and continue on behind Aaron as he turns north-east, heading into light coastal scrub.

We have brief glimpses of the coast through straggly vegetation as we make our way up and over Menzies Bluff. I am hoping the path allows for clearer views over the ocean soon, as I'd hate to miss seeing a boat. The descent will take us down to the beach, but first we have a few kilometres of steeper terrain and bush to push through. At times the path is obscured due to overgrown vegetation. There have obviously not been any recent walking parties ahead of us to push aside branches and cobwebs growing over the path. Aaron sets a slow, steady pace, which suits me fine as my legs feel heavy and my boat shoes slip and slide on the muddy track as we forge ahead.

Consciously walking in such a way as to conserve energy, and now that I'm more confident of my passage, I relax into the hike. Birdcall is prolific and the buzz of insects creates a cacophony of bush sounds. A hacking cough brings Aaron to a stop and he doubles over, hands on knees.

'Just my morning cough,' he splutters, seeing my concerned frown.

I am glad of the rest, as it's hard-going. Aaron stays bent over for long minutes and his cough sounds sinister. His health is concerning me more and more, and yet he insists he is fine. He sure does not sound it. Standing upright once the coughing has subsided, Aaron wipes a hand across his face and resumes walking.

I focus on placing one foot in front of the other, attuned to my immediate surroundings as I avoid tree roots that are a trip hazard and branches that spring back as Aaron pushes through vegetation ahead of me. Snakes generally move aside long before being seen in the bush, but just to be sure I herald my approach by brushing bushes with my stick. I am reminding myself of bush strategies after spending many months working and being on boats, and precious little time hiking. After recent events, my head feels a little detached from my body and my movements are clumsier than usual, as if brain signals are slightly delayed. Mistakes are easily made, and I'll be damned if I will make one at this stage.

Although the scrub is thick, there are areas where the forest does open up, providing window views over the water. I find myself enjoying the scenery and the exertion required to hike. Stick swishing and tap-tapping to the rhythm of the bush, sweat trails from my hairline, pools behind my ears, and runs down my cleavage. Huffing and puffing as we crest the knoll, our words are limited and breathing laboured.

After a brief rest and drink, we start making our way downhill, grabbing bushes for support as we lean back into the bluff, keeping our feet wide for balance. Half-sliding, I keep low to the ground, wary after falling off the tree branch earlier. Our descent is far quicker than the climb up Menzies Bluff. Fearing I will topple my companion if I fall against him, I try to keep distance between us as we make rapid progress to the outlet of Grotto Creek at the west end of Prion Beach. Here we pause to scoop up water from the creek. My face is slick with perspiration. Cupping water in my hands, I squat by the creek and splash behind my neck, getting instant relief. My shoes push into mud that sucks at my soles, and the air is thick with the drone of insects. Mosquitos buzz insistently around my face and I hasten across stones at the creek outlet.

We have reached Prion Beach.

Having passed my own test of sorts – not falling over in my boat shoes on the climb over Menzies Bluff – I skip along the low tide mark of the shoreline. Firm sand preferable to the soft stuff, walking here is easier and we are able to look beyond our feet as we continue forward. Precipitous Bluff provides an inspiring backdrop over the vast stretch of beach. Waves roll into shore, gulls circle, and the sun plays hide and seek with scattered clouds. To be in this environment, while making progress towards home, buoys my mood.

Precipitous Bluff is dominant as we stride along the beach. It is a formidable mountain, rising above the deep blue inland ranges, her summit touching wispy clouds. Humidity presses in on us as the sun reaches its apex on what is a glorious day. Halfway along the beach Aaron squats, takes out his tobacco pouch, and rolls a cigarette. Plonking onto the sand beside him, I study his profile. Thinning strands of greying hair flick around his face and a sudden rush of wind scuttles tiny shells. Like when young men chest bump in celebration, the shells rise up, meet and then fall away. Aaron looks overheated, even more so than I feel.

'Fancy a swim?' I suggest.

Aaron shakes his head. 'Change coming,' he muses, looking at the sky. 'We haven't got time to dawdle, regardless of this bloody humidity.'

Unfolding himself, he pushes back his flyaway hair and continues his steady progress along the beach.

Wiping away sweat, it's tempting to stay resting as I watch Aaron's outline recede, the beach slowly swallowing him. He is all arms and legs, encased in black shorts and hiking tights and a black t-shirt. It makes me feel even hotter looking at his attire. His long limbs seem to move through the air of their own accord, although nothing is rushed; his trunk upright and set forward. He really is an intriguing character.

Sighing, my body languid under the midday sun, I stand, brush sand from my legs, and prepare to jog up the beach and join Aaron. It is then that I notice red stains at my ankles. Pulling up my pant legs, I see two little suckers: leeches. Their bulbous black bodies are sated on my blood. Our stop at the creek gave opportunity for insects and leeches to feast on my flesh. A flick is all it takes to rid them from my body, gorged as they are.

Holding onto the other end of my sausage backpack, I jog along the sand towards Aaron and New River Lagoon. Beautiful environments rarely fail to instil feel-good endorphins in me, no matter what the circumstances, and as I make footprints in the sand I draw in the intoxicating smell of sea and salt, with just a hint of marijuana. A smoke trail, twirling like cotton off a spool, stretches behind Aaron.

Skipping over a small jellyfish wobbling close to the tideline, waiting for backwash, I look seawards. There, clear as day, is a fishing boat!

Shrugging the sling off my back, I frantically struggle to untie the knotted ends around my middle. Finally releasing the high-vis sheet from its cocoon, I flick it up and down, again and again.

'Help, look here!' I shout, running along the beach, throwing the neon sheet over my shoulders like a cape as it flutters awkwardly behind me.

Aaron turns and stands transfixed on the sand ahead of me, watching the fishing boat as it motors steadily eastwards.

'Grab a flare, Aaron,' I cry urgently.

He does not move, nor utter a word. My breath comes in ragged gasps as I stop to star jump on the spot, shouting louder, screeching into the wind that is picking up waves and racing away. 'Help, help!'

Throwing the high-vis sheet on the ground, I grapple to find a flare amongst my scattered belongings. When I do pick one up it immediately drops from my hands and rolls towards the water. I race to retrieve it and am overwhelmed with frustration as I look up in time to see the fishing boat's stern kick up white water. It becomes a smudge on the horizon as it races away as if in pursuit of fish or with an agenda to keep.

On my knees I weep, my happy mood gone as quickly as the boat had appeared then disappeared again. Aaron's arms come around me as he sinks onto his knees behind me, pulling me back against his greasy jumper smelling of man, animal, the bush, and sea. I long to be in Sam's arms, safely entwined under our pretty red and green doona aboard *Mulwala*. When Sam pulls my body into his, as he does nightly when spooning me to sleep, I always feel like I am in the safest place in the world; that whatever the problems of the day, all will be okay. Aaron's arms remind me of what I am missing most. He is not Sam, though, and I feel crushed by dark emotion. Wiping my snotty nose with the back of my hand, I push Aaron away from me.

'Bloody hell, Aaron, why didn't you help me?'

'No point, too far away.' He stands abruptly and retraces his steps towards the lagoon.

# UNDERTOW

My heaving chest gradually slows. Bowing my head to rest in upturned hands, my weeping softens. An image of my children, Matt and Sasha, comes to mind. We were holidaying in Port Douglas, a long way up the east coast of mainland Australia. Matt was celebrating his eighteenth birthday. He and Sasha had taken a walk together, brother and sister. Looking out the window of our palm and hibiscus-fronted apartment, I saw them running homewards through a tropical downpour, drenched and without a care in the world. Laughter carried through the driving rain, a happy, crazy, high-on-life sound, louder than the rain itself.

*When will I see them again? Does anyone know that I'm missing, or is it assumed that Sam and I are enjoying solitude and a well-earned break by ourselves at Cloudy Bay? Where is Sam, and why-oh-why hasn't he found me yet?*

twenty-one

# The lagoon

Minute sand particles sting my face and I squint to protect my eyes from the sudden onslaught. A fierce wind is whipping up sand along the beach and as I raise my head, I see billowing white plumes lift off the water as if a giant vacuum is sucking at the waves as they crest. The effect is stunning. Resembling a long piece of ripped gauze, a diaphanous sheet is suspended above the shoreline wave break. Huge waves are rolling towards land from the south.

The wind is accelerating, picking up momentum as it roars towards us. Aaron has run to my side and is hastily securing items in the sling. Now my gear is safely enfolded in my makeshift backpack, he quickly ties the end of the sheet into a firm knot at my front.

'Let's go, Kay – we've got to hurry,' he calls over his shoulder as he trots away.

I hold on to my hat as I run, half crouched against the force of the squall, to catch up with Aaron. I try to match his pace, and we link arms to prevent ourselves from toppling over. My hat is ripped off my head and I watch as it cartwheels along the beach, quickly lost. The famed Roaring Forties are challenging us. How quickly the weather has changed! We brace ourselves as we come closer together, hip to hip, forming a more solid wall against the elements. It's as if there is a giant in the sky blowing out big gusts of air, like the bully in the playground trying to bowl over the little kids.

New River Lagoon will not be visible until we round sand dunes at the eastern end of Prion Beach. Progress is hampered against the onslaught of wild weather. I feel like a character in a comic book; wobbling unsteadily, body bent sideways, and face contorted. For some reason I think it's hilarious, battling a force so strong. I imagine what we must look like and struggle not to laugh lest I cop a mouthful of sand. In contrast, Aaron's face is intent, all seriousness as he focuses on forward progress and practically drags me along.

Digging our toes into the soft sand, our calf muscles are stretched taut as we inch towards the end of the beach. We progress in increments, despite sometimes losing ground as we are buffeted about. With relief we finally turn inland across the sandbar that stretches out to meet the lagoon and aim for low, vegetated dunes that will provide us with some shelter from the wind and sand that slaps at our legs relentlessly. Making it to the sand dunes, we thrust our way into low lying bushes, scratches unheeded. The bushes pull at our skin and clothes as the wind tugs at the shrubbery, but it is a relief not to be in the open.

Aaron's face is grey, yet his eyes remain steely with determination. Despite his mental strength, it is becoming apparent that whatever ails him physically is taking its toll. Current conditions are not helping. He squats with his head between his knees, coughing up thick globules of spit which stain the sand at his feet. Alarmingly, his spittle has a pinkish tinge.

'Is that blood?' I ask, voice high.

'We have more pressing concerns, Kay,' he responds wearily before another coughing fit takes hold.

It is my turn to assist him and, ignoring the bushes that claw at me, I crawl behind Aaron to wrench his backpack off his shoulders. Sweat runs down the many lines and crevices of his face and his shirt is drenched in perspiration. Aaron's coughing subsides and we both slump heavily. Any attempt at conversation is hampered by the howling gale. Adrenaline still pumps around my body from the shock of the sudden change in weather, and we peer through the bushes as we pass a water bottle between us. Eddies skip across the tannin-stained waters of the lagoon. I remember the chocolate I have in my grab bag. I retrieve it and break off a couple of squares for each of us. We are grateful for the rest.

'This weather will get worse before it blows over,' Aaron states, voice raised over the wind.

I know he's right. The decision then is to try and find somewhere to set up shelter on this side of the lagoon or make a run for it – so to speak – and attempt to get to the sheltered campsite on the northern side of the waterway. The campsite is set further inland and will offer better protection than here, and it has a good water supply from Milford Creek. There is no way we can walk across the river mouth in any conditions, given what I have read of currents and freak waves, yet the idea still crosses my mind; it is obviously the narrowest point at which to cross. From where we are currently, the bank on the opposite side looks to be a long way away, and the wide waterway gives me a sense of foreboding. Conditions are worsening, and the crossing by boat will only get more hazardous as the day progresses.

'I'm really nervous of going into that,' I inform Aaron, pointing at the river.

'I know this weather. Soon there will be a lull as the weather system shifts. It's then that we need to go, and go quickly,' he replies, holding my wide-eyed stare.

Aaron's colouring has improved as he pushes forward with his argument, fearing we could get stuck on this side of the lagoon for days if we don't move. 'I need to get to the other side today, where there is more shelter,' he adds.

I look at him with a dawning understanding. The bloody spit is now a pressing concern.

'Okay, that makes sense. Can we wait till morning before bringing a dinghy back to this side though, given that the wind should have calmed a bit by then?' I ask.

'No hiker wants to be responsible for another not being able to reach shelter, Kay'

'Oh, so you reckon there is someone behind us in this?'

'Kay, it has to be done – bushman's law. I know my abilities.'

'Bloody hell, Aaron, we haven't seen anyone for days!'

I suggest waiting for a few hours to see what the wind will do, but Aaron is adamant we have to go soon or conditions could worsen. The wind has moderated a little, and so we decide to sit and wait; a compromise of sorts.

It is an hour before the bushes stop whipping us in the face and sand settles on the ground, rather than blowing in jet streams above us. Aaron assures me we will be protected from whatever the weather gods throw at us in the campground. Peaks rise on the water of the lagoon as it rushes inland towards Precipitous Bluff. Although the crossing looks scary, the shelter on the north side of the lagoon is enticing.

'I'm still nervous about this,' I bemoan. But I know that I can do little for Aaron on this side of the lagoon, and am starting to fear for both of our lives if we don't get help soon. Besides, the wind has dropped; it is now or we'll be stuck here for the night, and maybe tomorrow, too. Decision made, Aaron and I gather our belongings and make our way to the dinghy.

Aaron has convinced me that he is rested and can confidently row us across the lagoon. He holds the oars as I shove the dinghy into the water, then clamber aboard. Stowing our gear under the seats, we angle the dinghy towards the mouth of the lagoon; we will be working against wind and water and must use every advantage not to be swept inland. When we turn the boat at around the halfway mark, we should then have the wind's assistance to make it to the other shore without being pushed beyond the campground.

As Aaron rows sure and strong, hope fuels me – he is an excellent oarsman. I will have my turn when needed, if Aaron actually agrees to let go of possession of them.

The southwards sky is bruised violet, the dark horizon illuminated as the sun pierces through a heavy cloud bank. A rain front is looming, threatening clouds on a path towards Precipitous Bluff and the Southern Ranges.

We reach the far shore safely and I scamper up the bank to secure our belongings under bushes. After I have safely tied the second dinghy close behind us, we begin our row back across the lagoon. Despite the eerie drop in wind, it is harder going now. I can see Aaron is fatigued but he does not falter, muscles stretched taught, twitching with exertion. The rushing water is a mighty opponent. His rowing experience has come to the fore. One more trip and we will be able to set up camp away from this wind.

We reach the far shore and Aaron's head falls. His exhaustion is evident, and he struggles for breath. I untie the second dinghy and with all the muscle I can muster, haul it up the beach and secure it.

'Move, Aaron. I can take over the rowing for the last crossing.' I pick up the discarded oars from the bottom of the dinghy. He is incapable of argument. Aaron drops his head between his knees. His skin is the colour of old teabags. He sags back onto the floor.

There is an intensity in the air, as if the very sky is waiting for a cue to let loose. There is no time to wait. I suck in my stomach, press heels hard into the timber floor, and feel the muscles between my shoulder blades burn as I pull back on the oars.

# UNDERTOW

Angling the dinghy towards the mouth of the lagoon, I start to make progress as I replicate the direction Aaron had taken. The boat is lighter now we are not towing a second dinghy, but I'm struggling against the pull of weighted water, the current strong. My muscles scream in protest as I inch forward, passing the halfway point of the lagoon.

The wind howls like a banshee as we emerge from the eye of the storm and the full force of the front hits. In moments the lagoon resembles a thrashing brown snake, intent on slithering inland to seek shelter under the cover of Precipitous Bluff. The dinghy reaches the centre of the lagoon and is jolted. Gasping, I look up to see a frightening rush of water funnelling through the lagoon mouth and feel a sharp tug on the starboard oar. Aaron lunges across the dinghy and our hands meet. We both fight for possession of the oar and then it is gone, jarred out of its holder, swiftly lost to churning waters.

The stern of the dinghy swings hard away from the river mouth, and for precarious seconds we teeter, water sloshing over the boat's gunnels. Aaron grabs the remaining oar from me and tries to push the nose of the dinghy towards the far shore once more. He paddles furiously, first on one side of the boat and then swinging the oar in an arc, drives in deeply on the other side. His shoulders buck with effort. Dazed, one hand on either side of the boat, I see that the effort is too much for Aaron and the dinghy is starting to be sucked upriver, my weight in the bow not helping. If I attempt to change positions the boat may tip precariously, so I hold on, rooted to the spot.

My instincts scream at me to take action before our situation becomes even more perilous. We have been swept up river a couple of hundred metres and the campground – and our belongings – are behind us. Confusion and fear give way to fight or flight instincts as it suddenly becomes crystal clear what I need to do, for my life and for Aaron's. Away from the deep middle of the lagoon-turned-river with its rush and suck, I know I have a good chance of making it. I am a strong swimmer and have had professional training in my triathlon days. Without my weight, Aaron will have a better chance of getting the dinghy, and himself, ashore.

I yell my intention to leap overboard and don't wait for a reply. Without hesitation, I dive over the side as far away from the dinghy as I can. Darkness engulfs me as the cold slap of water stings my body. I know I will remember this moment forever, if I survive. I swim through darkness, the weight of water pressing against me and pulling at my legs.

It is said that there is a moment in life when everything changes. I have not endured all I have to die at this point. I surface and gulp in fresh air, my arm raised towards the deep indigo sky. Turning face down I stretch and pull back against the water, much as I had with the oars only short minutes ago. Legs kicking hard from my hips, my body responds to what I ask of it.

There's light below me. I dolphin kick through the shallow water. Muscle memory takes over and I'm up and running as soon as my feet touch sand. I am immune to fingernail-sharp branches scratching at my legs as I leap over shoreline shrubbery. I can see Aaron in my peripheral vision, closer to the water's edge now, around twenty metres downstream from me. His movements are frenzied, the oar slicing left and right, never faltering as he fights to break from the push of water northwards. Running through the knee-high shallows, I dive once more and in half a dozen strokes have reached the dinghy. I grasp the metal ring at the bow then get a firm hold of the painter line – a rope for towing – which is threaded through the ring. I turn and kick towards the shoreline. Aaron works with me, challenging the rushing flow. The dinghy scrapes against sand.

Tying the rope securely around a sturdy shrub set back from the shoreline, I step back into the dinghy and fall into Aaron's arms. Sobbing, we cling to each other, our drenched clothing adhering us as one. Time slows. Aaron's bony chest heaves against mine as his lungs struggle to find air.

'It's okay,' I whisper, 'it's okay.'

I'm not sure if I'm reassuring Aaron or myself.

twenty-two

# Maz

The bruised clouds look like bunches of purple grapes after a good stomping. I shiver violently as I rifle through my bags, then hastily strip off my sodden clothes and pull on my thermals. The upper branches of trees lay horizontal in strong gusts, and I'm relieved to be in the sheltered campground, which is nestled beyond the tree line. I quickly set up Aaron's tent, ensure it is secure, then inflate his sleeping mat and lay out the sleeping bag.

Coughs rack Aaron's body as I help him to untie his boots and set them outside the tent. Protected from the wind in the tent's confines, Aaron pulls his wet shirt over his head. I can't help but notice the wastage of his body and how each rib protrudes. I turn away as Aaron pulls on his thermal top then drags himself awkwardly into the sleeping bag. He draws the down cover up to his chest and rolls on his side to grope through his belongings that are scattered untidily around us. Finding his tobacco pouch and fumbling with it, marijuana leaves pick up and blow around the tent in little flurries. I gently ease the pouch from his cold fingers.

'I'll roll the joint for you. Get warm and I'll be back to you in a few moments.'

He sighs and lies down in answer. I crawl out of the tent, tobacco pouch in hand.

Squatting with my back to the wind in imitation of Aaron, I try vainly to keep the tobacco inside the paper. Fumbling, the small task becomes an enormity I struggle to deal with. I want to scream, to lie down somewhere soft, and to eat – all are of equal priority. But overriding anything I desire is Aaron's need of the medicinal properties of marijuana. Now, more than ever, I long to give him that comfort.

'Here, let me help you.'

The voice startles me and I yelp in surprise. Wondering if I am delusional, I can only stare dumbly.

There is a woman standing in front of me. She looks real enough as she laughs and beckons for me to hand her the tobacco. Our hands meet and I know with certainty that this is not an apparition, but an actual person in front of me.

'I'm tempted to ask for a roach, but it looks like your friend needs it more than me.'

She indicates the tent with a nod of her head and a wry smile. Her Canadian accent is evident and she looks sure of herself, dark eyes merry. Where she has come from, I do not know. Perhaps her tent is sheltered behind trees. She rolls the joint deftly.

'Thank you,' I say, adding hopefully, 'any chance you have an EPIRB?'

She shakes her head. I sigh deeply as I lean into the tent and hand the joint to Aaron.

He has his lighter at the ready and, with the first drag, eases his head back against a bunched-up coat. Almost instantly he sits up again as he succumbs to hawking. He is embarrassed as I hand him a water bottle, which he accepts with shaking hands. My concerns mount. I put the back of my hand against his cheek. He feels cold and clammy. I wish I could pour him a shot of whisky.

'Don't fret, Kay. Just let me rest and go and take care of yourself,' he says croakily.

It's a relief to hear him talking. I smile. 'Okay, take it easy for a bit. Get some shut-eye.'

Aaron takes my hand and grips it tightly for a moment, his eyes on mine. I know he is silently thanking me.

With her back resting comfortably against a tree and legs akimbo in front of her, the woman is sitting close by smoking a cigarette. She pats the ground beside her and I sit heavily, weary to the bone. Wind shakes the branches above us and leaves rain down. She holds out the cigarette to me.

'What the heck,' I say with a shrug, reaching for it.

'This packet is for emergencies only,' she says with a wink, shaking the cigarettes in front of me. 'Honestly, I could not believe it when I saw the both of you rowing over the lagoon.' Grinning, she leans forward and appraises me with sharp eyes. 'I'm Maz. You should rest, too. It'll be raining again soon. Use my tent. I'll keep an eye on your friend.'

'Thanks for your help,' I say with a small smile. 'I'm Kay, and my friend is Aaron. He's sick. I need to get help. Is there anyone else here? I'm desperate to get my hands on an EPIRB or sat phone.'

'Nobody in the last few days, and I was the only one here before you two showed up.'

Maz appears genuinely concerned and yet has a robust confidence that is reassuring. There are so many questions I want to ask her, as I am sure she does me, but the thought of an hour or two's sleep not only sounds like bliss, but is a necessity.

'I'll take you up on that offer, but can you please wake me if someone rocks up or you see a helicopter?'

'Of course. It's obvious you two need help. You can tell me all about it after some shut-eye.'

*Wow, the gods have sent Aaron and I some help in the form of this bubbly woman.*

She leads me to a nearby fire pit where she has a small fire going. Maz's dark hair is tied back in a messy ponytail that trails down her back between muscled shoulders. She radiates energy and purpose, and even though she must obviously have hiked a long way to get here, she looks a lot fresher than Aaron or I.

I huddle as close as I can to the fire, hands outstretched, grateful beyond words for the warmth. Maz hands me a water bottle and I take small sips from it as the heat of the fire penetrates through my thermals. She throws some sticks onto the fire. I smile in appreciation. My instincts tell me Maz is the real deal. 'Please keep that going and I'll help you to build it up when I've had a breather.'

My head is fuzzy, mind and body shutting down after the shock of recent events. My stomach is flip-flopping, and I tell myself I will whip up a proper meal for Aaron and myself once I've closed my eyes for a bit.

Maz stands. 'I'll check on your friend. My tent is that-a-way.' She points to the far side of the campground.

It is a large campground, sites hidden behind trees and well-placed. Maz appears undaunted by the weather as she strides to Aaron's tent, her functional hiking pants tight across her butt, ponytail flicking side to side. Leaves, twigs, and debris swirl around her legs as they dance across the campground. Willy-willies are growing in front of me, gusts picking up leaf matter to send them funnelling upwards in mini tornadoes. I'm trembling, body depleted, cold taking a hold as fat rain drops start to fall, smacking me in the face.

My legs have become numb when Maz reappears beside me, reassuring me that Aaron is okay. She helps me stand upright and leads me forwards. Dark spots appear in front of my eyes, bile rises, and I vomit. I heave up repeatedly, purging myself of the brown river. Maz supports me as my body shakes uncontrollably. Throwing my head back, I open my mouth to drink the rain. The tree canopy leans protectively over us as the sky erupts, and lightning tears holes in heavy clouds no longer able to hold back their contents. Blasts of thunder assault us. Maz still has her arm around me as she leads me to her tent and unzips the fly. The moment I lie down, I feel myself slipping into sleep.

Registering the light pitter-patter of rain on nylon, I wake. Clenching and unclenching my sore hands – *what doesn't ache?!* – I am happy to doze. Rain falls with a steady insistence on the tent and I snuggle further down into the warm sleeping bag, a comforting arm draped loosely over me.

Sleep still hangs heavily as I lift one eyelid. Maz's arm is an easy weight, relaxed in sleep. Her hand lies beside me, feminine despite unkempt nails, fingers long like a pianist. It feels wonderful to be warm and dry, to hear the tent rustle in the wind and rain-muffled sounds; to feel cared for, to feel safe. After all I have been through, I will accept the good without question. I give in to a dreamless state as the storm assaults the outside world, animals in hiding, humans in their nylon shelters, buffeted but to beat to care.

When next I open my eyes, I take a moment to register where I am. Maz kisses my shoulder. The surprise of this simple action is lessened by the circumstances. Emotions are either heightened or dulled in times of shock, grief, or pain. My overwhelming need for human touch negates all else. In t-shirt and knickers only, I press back against Maz, tucking my bottom into her stomach. I groan involuntarily with the pleasure of feeling warm flesh, too long denied me through harrowing ordeals. Locked in this sheltered world, there is only the here and now.

Picking up Maz's hand, I kiss the hollow between her thumb knuckle and index finger. I want her to know my appreciation, and, to be honest, to feel tenderness in turn. I have been through so much and have had to be stronger than I could ever have imagined. And I have done it mostly on my own. Now Aaron is ill. I don't want to think and I don't want to be alone. My eyes are closed as I turn to her.

Skin slides against skin as my shirt rides up. Resting my head against Maz's chest, I recall Sam's love of my nipples. Small breasts highlight nipples, and Sam loves how mine grow under his teasing tongue. Lowering my head, my hair sweeps over Maz's breasts, fuller than my own but equally responsive to touch. I listen to Maz's heartbeat, as steady as the beat on our nylon enclosure. Her hand slides down my back with a feather-like touch. She turns, ever so slightly, her breast rolling under my cheek. My lips meet her soft flesh. Exploring with my tongue, I know the texture and smooth skin of another woman's breast.

I have wondered often, as I am sure most women do, why men are so fascinated with breasts – Freudian theory aside. Now I know why, firsthand. As Maz's rounded breasts thrust against me, I press my lips against her collarbone, tasting her neck as my hand rises to cup each breast in turn.

Hungrier, I pull sharply on one nipple before covering it with my mouth. Teasing the nipple, tongue darting in and out, I let my fingers roam over Maz's body. She is naked bar knickers, and as I apply pressure on her buttocks to draw her towards me, my fingers slide cloth aside. Maz gasps then puts her hands behind my head and pulls my mouth to hers. Her hands then trace my hip bones and slide down between my legs, artfully and with a knowing touch. Thoughts tumbling, images of Sam merge with the touch of this woman as I drink in the taste, the togetherness, the matching hunger of another.

twenty-three
# Reunion Island

Unexpected gifts give double the pleasure.

In 2016 Sam and I moved into our beach house on Tasmania's east coast so that Sam could pursue a dream skippering role in the area. My heart was heavy as we left our yacht on a mooring and farewelled the boating community and a lifestyle I had embraced. Our land- based move coincided with a chaotic and uncertain period in our lives. I hoped the calm of our new surrounds would help my writing aspirations; however, I was loathe to leave our dream of sailing into the sunset behind.

I had been living at the beach house for some months and had been unsettled and missing life on the water when a friend suggested a week's holiday on Reunion Island. Jane liked to hike and was always on the lookout for interesting destinations – much as I am – where she could either jump on her bike or pull on her hiking boots. The beach house I was living in was directly by the water and in a picturesque environment. While it was a perfect setting in which to write, it did not provide me with the stimulation I had become accustomed to when living on a yacht. Hence, I readily accepted Jane's invitation.

From Johannesburg – where she was working at the time – it was only around four hours flight time to get to Reunion, while for me it would take two days of travel to get there. I had my ticket booked within hours regardless, as the island sounded exotic and the perfect antidote to a bout of the doldrums.

Reunion Island is French-owned, a tiny jewel sitting out in the Indian Ocean, with its nearest neighbour being the better known, and more populous, Mauritius Island. One of my greatest joys in life is exploring new environments and cultures. This hiking holiday was an unexpected gift that I treasure to present day.

On my arrival, Jane picked me up from Roland Garros Airport – the main airport on the island – in a little Citroen car she had hired. It proved a reliable car, and just as well because soon we would be navigating the treacherous inland roads to commence hiking in the most inaccessible region on the island.

Being a lesser visited travel destination, in part due to its remote location, Reunion Island is most famous for Piton de la Fournaise, which is one of the most active volcanoes on Earth. As luck would have it, on our first day on the island we picked up a newspaper and discovered that the volcano was erupting, as it does on a regular basis (usually, at least once a year). Jane was keen to go and see it. I was a little unsure; an erupting volcano sounded a tad dangerous.

'Didn't we come here for adventure?' queried Jane. 'Anyway, they wouldn't let us near the place if it was life-threatening.' Her arguments were valid, and so we fired up the Citroen and headed south.

Walking across a lunar-like landscape, we were rewarded with a technicolour light show of sparks shooting into the sky and lava spewing forth from gaping holes in the Earth's surface. As the craters and spatter cones inside the caldera routinely ejected fiery contents, I made sure to stick to the trail. My introduction to Reunion Island was a hot-footed one as we followed a crowd of curious onlookers around the caldera. Gendarmes maintained a casual order, and ambulances and fire trucks stood by baking in the afternoon sun just in case they should be required. It was all very laidback. Locals familiar with the event came armed with picnic hampers. Just as back home a circus or annual show is something communities look forward to, for the residents of Reunion the eruption of Piton de la Fournaise was eagerly anticipated.

We drove away from the blackened volcanic landscape that is a feature of the south-eastern corner of the island, pointing the little car inland. We were aiming to hike into the crater of Cirque de Mafate, which is the steepest of the three cirques on Reunion. Looking at a map I was reminded of a beehive, as the topography necessitates astounding switchback roads that zigzag up and down the mountainous landscape. The road has multiple twists and turns and dangerous gutters that drop off on either side. The closer we got to the cirque, the more we steeled ourselves for what lay ahead. A small gravelled carpark announced we had reached our destination.

Donning my backpack, I peered over the crater rim and struggled to see a track that would make the descent negotiable. Jane consulted the map. 'This way,' she indicated, dropping off the edge and out of sight.

We bravely set forth – well, Jane was brave and I simply followed her lead. During that long afternoon we covered a distance of around two kilometres, descending over a thousand metres into the heart of a collapsed volcano. It doesn't sound far, but as we didn't start walking until 2:00pm a brisk pace was necessary and I struggled to keep up with my companion.

'C'mon,' Jane called over her shoulder, a little impatiently.

It was at around that point that I told myself that I would train for my next adventure.

'Okay, I'll try and pick up the pace,' I panted as I watched Jane disappear around the next bend.

The sun was sinking towards the crater rim and shadow quickly swallowed the valley floor. Wary of cobwebs as lethal as fishing wire, we swept aside vegetation that encroached on the trail while the dogs howled day's end. Giant orb spiders were silhouetted against the dim light of dusk, reminding me of a scene from a *Jurassic Park* movie. I gained extra motivation and hurried forth, as eager as Jane to make it to the *gite* – hostel – by nightfall.

Finally reaching our destination of Roche Plate, we stumbled into the Thomas Juliette gite. Collapsing onto a bunk, I could barely nod, let alone talk. As hungry as I was and despite knowing dinner was a communal affair – something I would normally enjoy – I was unable to drag myself off my bunk. For some time, I was only vaguely aware of my surrounds, of people and evening activity around me. I am unsure how long I sat there before I was able to move again.

Hiking into an ancient volcanic crater required a descent down a gradient that favoured the likes of mountain goats. Yet people live in these valleys, accessible by foot or helicopter only. Many of the valley's inhabitants are the descendants of runaway slaves and are no doubt a resilient people – and what a worthy refuge Mafate is. I, on the other hand, could have been knocked over with a feather at that point.

When I had recovered a little, I became aware of a woman sitting beside a child in a bunk opposite mine, crooning softly in a lilting French accent. Her voice had a balm-like quality and worked for me like a lullaby; perhaps it was. I fell back on my bunk and slept more soundly than I had done for many a year.

As a rooster crowed, I slid out of my bunk quietly, not wanting to disturb my snoring roommates. Walking out onto the deck, I was witness to the sun rising in one of the most astounding natural environments I have ever seen. I strained my neck to look upwards and trace where I had descended from the day prior, staring in disbelief at the sheer rockface that loomed behind the gite. The mountain was still in shadow and while it looked intimidating, even menacing, I was at that stage blissfully unaware of the torment heat reflected off rock can create. I could only marvel as the sun rose and the light washed over the valley walls. It was an otherworldly scene. Reunion Island is unique on this earth.

Padding quietly across the floorboards, I walked to the railing. A golden shaft of light pointed over the crater rim, the effect like a spotlight being shone directly into my eyes. As the light grew and travelled, I took in all around me. Now the valley looked like the Garden of Eden, lush and bountiful. I could well have gone up the Faraway Tree and through the clouds to new lands. Instead, I had descended into an ancient volcano where I discovered my version of paradise and Mother Nature ruled.

Volcanic earth is rich in nutrients, and in a moist environment plant and insect life grow in oversized proportions. Jane joined me on deck with mugs of tea and together we revelled in the rewards of our labours from the previous day. In a few short hours the sun would scald the mountaintop and slide in a hot rush to the valley floor below. Before that, Jane and I would eat our breakfast sitting on the deck, feet on the railing and hearts full from the blessings of Mother Nature. Palm fronds, large and glossy, waved at us, and birds sang from within the green oasis before us. Jane made me a second cup of tea and together we feasted on a breakfast of porridge in a dining room fit for kings, the valley our richly adorned palace.

Extremes – of environment and circumstances – test us. On Reunion Island I faced many challenges and was rewarded with a sense of peace and tranquillity that I have rarely experienced.

I pushed my body harder than I had for over a decade and it was worth every blistering step. Waking in Cirque de Mafate was a sublime experience. I have learnt that the opposing forces of chaos and tranquillity are not as far apart as we may imagine. The trick is to hang in there and, in doing so, gain great rewards.

twenty-four
# Aftermath

Dawn eases into day, the warble of honeyeaters and caw of currawongs clear under a blue sky. As I walk from Maz's tent to Aaron's, I gaze around at bush washed clean. The Prion Beach campsite is vast, leaf litter creating a soft floor interrupted only by fallen sticks and branches that have been whipped into piles, a reminder of last night's strong winds. Peppermint gums and linear stringybarks stand sentinel over the campground. Slumbering after a stormy night, white puffball clouds are docile on a blue palette. Nature is celebrating a new day, as am I.

A leaf brushes my shoulder and spirals to ground. A memory of Maz's finger tracing a line down my arm sends a shiver of pleasure through me. We had lain side by side in her tent, our bodies fused together in the nylon enclosure as darkness slid away and we talked in whispers. She was astounded to hear of Sam's strange disappearance and of my survival after *Mulwala* had floundered and sank. I told her of my connection to Sam and how I felt he was still alive.

'The heart knows what it knows,' Maz had replied. I smile as I remember her wise words. It was then that she had vowed to help me, and Aaron, anyway she could. Asking if Aaron had shown signs of ill health before yesterday's events, I replied that I guessed he was not a well man but was in the dark regarding his medical condition.

'He acknowledged that he has a broken heart, not what's going on with his physical health,' I told Maz. We concurred that whatever was ailing him appeared to be serious.

Inland, low clouds cling to the upper reaches of Precipitous Bluff. Thick forest flanks the mountain's sheer sides and rocky peaks snap at the sky. It is a majestic mountain, both formidable and alluring. The path to it involves a wade northward up New River Lagoon before hikers can tread on firm ground again. I have read it is a challenging hike, rewarding those who make it to the summit of the mountain.

'What will today bring?' I ask a currawong hopping close to me. It looks at me with head tilted to one side and yellow eyes bright with interest, despite having no answer for me.

I give silent thanks for the positioning and protection of the campground. Here we had avoided full exposure to the storm. Despite our misfortune in the dinghy, I cannot help but wonder how Aaron would have survived in the more open scrub on the other side of the lagoon (or myself for that matter). The onslaught of the storm has affected both the physical environment and Aaron's health. In its aftermath, conditions have altered; Aaron's health has become my priority.

It is a relief to see Aaron sitting on the ground outside his tent, gazing into the distance in his customary pose of elbows resting on knees. He is all angles, long limbs folding into his thin frame. I give a wave as I approach, determined to have a conversation with him about his health. Maz is right in concluding that Aaron needs to get back to Hobart as quickly as I do.

He gazes with steady attention as I near him. 'Morning, Kay.'

'You're looking better today.' I remark.

His response is a coughing fit. Aaron reaches for a water bottle and takes a swig, wiping his mouth with the back of his hand. 'As are you,' he states with a knowing smile.

I burst out laughing, surprising myself and a kookaburra that decides to add its voice to mine, cackling loudly in the tree above us. Aaron chortles and the bush comes alive with merry chorus. I have no regrets about my night with Maz. I'm recharged and helping Aaron is my first priority.

The laughter has done more to clear the air than the storm had. 'Aaron, what's wrong?' I ask, taking a risk and launching right in. 'I don't just mean the effects of the storm. I'm worried about you and I want to help.'

Nothing. I try again.

'Can you talk to me about it?'

'Let's go for a walk,' he replies.

'That sounds like a plan.' I take his arm to help him stand. 'We can chat as we go.'

As he stands, I note that he would have been a fine-looking man before illness reduced him. We slowly make our way towards the edge of the lagoon. There we find a log with bright orange fungi protruding from its base. We sit and Aaron wheezes, catching his breath, while I look on in concern. My alarm is heightened as he unwittingly puts his hands on his ribs and winces, quickly dropping his arms as he sees me watching him. His fatigue is pronounced and we have only walked twenty metres.

The lagoon is now a fast-moving river. I gaze out over the water, marvelling at the power of the Roaring Forties that can so quickly subside, leaving destruction in its wake. Mountain runoff has widened the waterway by a few metres, and the water is a tannin-rich brew infused with mud and debris. Rushing to escape to sea, the water sweeps all in its path along for the ride. Branches and vegetation are being tumbled around as the lagoon spits waste products out into the Southern Ocean.

I turn to Aaron and my gut clenches. His face is the colour of bleached timber. Although we made it across the lagoon, the risk we took came at a price; whatever ails Aaron has been exacerbated. He clears his throat, and with a resigned sigh starts to speak.

'Kay, I have seen a lot of doctors over many years for my head and for medical stuff. I've had enough. I know my lungs are stuffed. That's bloody obvious. I choose – do you hear me? – I *choose* to spend time out here. The bush heals. I've got medication with me. Don't worry. You just focus on getting home to your family. Okay?'

Aaron hunches his shoulders and drops his hands between his knees, exhausted from his speech. I am lost for words. Minutes pass before he lifts his eyes to search mine, wanting understanding, begging me to let him be.

'What if whatever is wrong is getting worse? You could die out here if you don't get checked out and treated properly,' I say, voice strained.

Aaron turns away from me, staring inland. His eyes follow the lagoons path. Picking up my hand, he rubs his thumb absently across my knuckles in a gesture of comfort.

'Let's rest today and think about things. You can build up your signal fire, talk to Maz. Remember our agreement to part here? Just focus on getting yourself home. Please, Kay.'

Seeing the resolve in his eyes, I throw my arms around Aaron's bony shoulders. He hugs me awkwardly in turn. His sharp elbows dig into my back.

'You are a stubborn man. Please think carefully. It is crazy to stay out here like this.' I say quietly. I know deep in my gut that it will be near impossible to get this proud man to change his mind.

Aaron assures me he will be okay to rest for a while where he is. Handing him my water bottle, I set off to check on the dinghy I secured after our epic water crossing. I need time to process the news that has been imparted. As I walk, I notice the stream of smoke in the air and silently thank Maz for building up the fire. Hoping my knot-tying skills have passed the test, I scramble through the low shrubbery that is half-submerged in brackish water. Relieved to find the dinghy still secure, I reach underwater to untie it from the trunk of a sturdy shrub. Yesterday it had stood alongside the boat, not in the water as it is now.

Towing the dinghy awkwardly downstream, I stick to the very edge of the fast-flowing water, carefully avoiding branches that are moving swiftly towards the lagoon entrance. I flip the boat upside-down with an almighty heave and fasten it securely. Doing something constructive is a relief. Grateful to see that a spare pair of oars is in a labelled container close by, I retrace my steps back towards Aaron.

Wading in the shallows, leaf matter and grit churned up by the current swirls around my legs. It is bewildering how savage storms are in this wilderness and hard to believe how quickly conditions can become life-threatening. As I get closer to Aaron, I think about the responsibility I feel for him. I can't just ditch a sick friend, no matter what he says.

Aaron is sitting where I left him, shoulders heaving from the effort of harsh coughing. Distressed to see sweat pouring out of him as he fights to breathe, I let rip a piercing whistle, silently thanking my dad for the skill (one learnt to round up cattle all the more readily). Maz hears me and is quick to join us.

'Geez, you don't look too good,' she says to Aaron as we help him to his feet.

Maz and I support him as we make our way back to the campground. It is slow going; every few feet we have to stop while Aaron sucks in air. Manoeuvring him into the tent, I help to prop him up on makeshift pillows while Maz runs to fetch fresh water.

Unable to speak, Aaron points to a pile of belongings heaped to one side of the tent. Rifling through clothing and other items, I find a large zip lock bag full of an array of medications. Alarmed by this new evidence of Aaron's chronic poor health, I hand the bag to him. He fumbles with packets of pills, finds the bottle he is looking for, and swallows some capsules. His barking cough gradually subsides and with relief he lies back, the rise and fall of his chest rapid.

Maz returns to the tent after fetching water from upstream. Aaron drinks thirstily.

'Fair dinkum, the storm has made a bit of a mess. Lots of branches down. It's a bitch getting upriver for fresh water,' Maz comments. Her Canadian accent gives the Aussie vernacular comical flair, and I see Aaron's mouth turn up slightly in appreciation. Good. He must be feeling a bit better.

Maz and I sit together on either side of Aaron, our eyes meeting briefly, each mirroring the concern of the other.

'Aaron, what can we do to help?' I ask.

Aaron turns his back to us, pulling the sleeping bag more closely around him. 'Just let me rest,' he mumbles. His breathing calms and he is quickly asleep.

With Maz close behind me, I lift up the tent flap and we make our way across the sun-speckled campsite to the shoreline.

'He's really sick, Maz. It's his lungs. He won't tell me what it is but I reckon he knows.' My voice carries the fear I feel. She drops an arm over my shoulder and gives me a brief hug. Weariness and concern are weighing me down and I gratefully accept Maz's offer of a mug of tea. I drag a decent sized log onto the fire as she makes a brew.

As the sun emerges intermittently from behind clouds, warmth infuses me. I wander down the shoreline towards the mouth of the lagoon. Scrambling up to the top of a sand dune, I look seawards. The swell is large after yesterday's fierce south-westerly blow and I watch as waves ride in long lines, sweeping across the ocean, no break in their journey. I listen to

# UNDERTOW

the soothing jabbering of oystercatchers on the shoreline. I look back and see Maz heading back beyond the tree line in search of dry wood.

The journey I have been on to get here seems surreal, and every day poses new challenges. My immediate priorities have shifted, much like the sand beneath my feet. Drawing a pattern in the sand with my toes, I then erase the swirls and indentations with a single swipe. As my daughter Sasha is wont to say, 'Life is messy.' I sigh. How right she is.

A squabble breaks out amongst the oystercatchers who are vying for a foreshore delicacy. Nature has a fickle disposition. Life goes on regardless. There may be slight variations, but the world still rotates and the sun still rises. The most fundamental things stay the same. It was only a few short weeks ago that I had left Hobart with Sam for a sailing holiday, happily anticipating fun adventures ahead. Then it all went to shit. If not for a myriad of accidents, incidents, and chance encounters, I would not be here now. My journey of survival has changed me profoundly, in ways I am not yet sure of. Standing, I brush the sand off my legs and start back towards the campground. I have wood to collect, and a helicopter landing pad to clear.

Maz emerges through the trees and hands me a fruit and nut bar. What a gift this woman is.

'Thanks, Maz. I'm going to need to clear an area for a rescue helicopter to land. They hate the sand.'

'Sounds great. I'll help in any way I can. I'm not going to continue my hike until I know you two are safe.'

My stomach grumbles but I have other priorities at present. A good meal will come soon enough. Maybe it will be in Hobart before nightfall. That thought gets me moving all the faster.

After checking on Aaron, who is sleeping soundly, Maz and I heap up the fire and then head to an exposed area of sand and start clearing it of debris for a makeshift helicopter landing pad.

We make sure the high-vis sheet is in a visible spot and secure it with large rocks. Logic tells me that after this period of time Hobart search and rescue will be aware that I am missing and a search will be imminent, if not already in progress. Having lost track of days, I know only that family and friends will be watching out for Sam's and my return.

Standing back to survey our handiwork, both Maz and I are pleased with our efforts. The fire has died down while we worked. It's hard to find dry wood. Maz and I split up and search for more fuel to ensure the fire is kept going.

Flames greedily consume a mound of dry leaves, red tongues reaching up to lick at a tepee of twigs as the fire gains intensity. In no time at all the fire is raging again. We throw off our filthy clothes and make our way to the beach. With shrieks, we dive in to the delightfully cold water, which hits like slap. My dreary mood dissipates as I dolphin dive, again and again.

As the afternoon wanes, Maz and I take it in turns to check on Aaron. His mouth hangs slack and the rise and fall of his chest is rapid, yet still he sleeps. We bring food down to the water, hungry after our exertions. Cooking up the last of the rice Yuto had given me, Maz surprises me with an offering of mussels she had found clinging to a rocky outcrop at Surprise Bay. This was the last campsite she had overnighted at, coming from the east before hiking to New River Lagoon. We save some precious rice and seafood for Aaron.

'I hope he eats something soon. He's only had sips of water today, as far as I can tell,' I confide.

'He won't refuse this feast,' declares Maz with an optimism I'm becoming accustomed to.

I wish I could be as optimistic. I had been so hopeful that today was the day rescue would come. Pooling together our resources, Aaron, Maz, and I now have an adequate food supply for a few days. Surely, help will come well before our supplies get low.

Maz and I converse easily, our rapport born of circumstance and shared passions. While we are eating Maz tells me stories about her childhood and growing up in Canada with wilderness as her playground. She goes on to tell me how she later became disillusioned with study, seeking adventure and travel. In turn I share childhood and travel tales, our stories not vastly dissimilar. Our mutual love of outdoors and adventure is obvious. I am gobsmacked to learn that Maz has spent twelve months in Central Australia – in Alice Springs – learning the art of tour guiding, as this is a course I too have considered.

Maz tells me she was quick to fall in love with Australia and its people. However, after several months she needed a change from the mainland's dry centre and craved greenery and ocean views. Tasmania beckoned. The South Coast Track was one she eagerly embarked upon after reading of its beauty and remoteness, much like Sam and I had done shortly after I had moved to Tasmania. Maz has secured a tour guiding job on the Freycinet Peninsula, to commence in the coming summer. She first plans to gain knowledge of Tasmania's remote national parks, on foot and in a kayak.

As Maz speaks, her irrepressible spirit shines through. I think how much Sam would like my new friends and my face must have dropped for, as if reading my mind, Maz takes my hand in hers.

'I am going to do all I can to help you and Sam be reunited, and to get Aaron help. They have to be looking for you now. We'll keep a big fire going all night.'

I smile, squeezing her hand. 'Thank you. For everything.'

We have formed a bond that I feel sure will endure. I love those women who can give so freely of themselves, in many respects – not least to care for others – and without obligation. Not all women, but certainly many I know of and many I have met in my life. For that fact, I hold deep gratitude.

The fire is bright at our backs, heavy timber now alight. The sun has gone down, the night clear and calm. A million stars wink back at me as I gaze up at the sky. Maz gives me a quick kiss and bids me goodnight. We will take it in turns to see to the fire throughout the night. I watch as Maz departs, then drag over another log, hefting it up onto the burning pile. Flames leap skywards and create a dazzling foreground to Precipitous Bluff, silhouetted in the moonlight.

twenty-five
# A mountain calls

I crawl into my sleeping bag by the fire and am immediately mesmerised by the white trail of the Milky Way. Stars wink boldly, and a streak of light plummets towards the earth and quickly disappears. I fall asleep and dream of stars merging and becoming a phosphorescent sea. I am drawn into that sea, and as I wade deeper, I scoop aside water that flows through my fingers and sparkles with life.

I am hitching a ride to the ocean's floor on the back of a whale when I am pulled into semi-wakefulness by Aaron's scouring cough. Keeping my eyes closed for precious minutes more, I hover on the edge of my dream.

Neptune greets me – bearing a striking resemblance to Aaron – and a mermaid with Maz's radiant smile weaves merrily around the whale and I. Clinging to the fanciful dream world where all things are possible, reality nonetheless prods me into wakefulness. Aaron's cough reverberates around the campground. I open my eyes reluctantly, pick up my sleeping bag, and shuffle towards Aaron's tent. Checking in on my friend, I see that he is fast asleep again despite his hacking. I retrieve my sleeping bag and lay it out nearby. The night will be long.

As morning dawns, I give up on all pretence of sleep and wearily make my way over to Maz, who is dragging an old log towards the fire. Together we upturn the log and tip it onto the fire heap, then turn our attention to making a cuppa. Aaron has slept long, despite his incessant coughing. He finally emerges from his tent, looks around, and then walks towards us. I hand him a mug of strong coffee laced heavily with sugar, which he accepts gratefully.

'Thanking you,' he mumbles, rubbing sleep from his eyes with the back of his hand.

'How are you feeling, mate?' asks Maz.

'Not bad. Be better after some tucker.'

'No wonder, you missed a good feed last night. Here you go.' Maz hands Aaron a plate of freshly caught fish.

Maz had utilised her time well while on fire watch, casting a fishing line into the lagoon at first light. She explains that she bought a lightweight fold-up fishing rod before her foray on the South Coast Track, in the hope of supplementing her diet of dehydrated food. It works a treat as she has caught several fish with the rod.

'This is my first trout,' she announces triumphantly.

With the small fishing line and only an insect for bait, Maz's catch would gain the respect and envy of many a fisherman; the flooded lagoon must have coughed up a fish or two. She is an impressive woman, of that there is no doubt.

Aaron picks at the fish, swallowing it down with a second mug of coffee. Although my concern for Aaron is growing, my appetite is not diminished and I set about eating my serve of the fish with relish.

A burnt orange sky dissolves into blue as the sun rises above the campground. Resting in his sleeping bag once more, Aaron's hacking startles a flock of black cockatoos that squawk loudly as they pass overhead.

Maz and I walk down to the shoreline. Trailing sand through our fingers as we sit, we rehash vague plans we made during the night. A part of me simply wants to start running and keep running until I reached Cockle Creek and can radio for help. Not very practical considering the country I would have to negotiate to do so.

'It makes the most sense for me to go in search of help,' Maz says.

'It does. I can't leave yet, as much as I want to get going. Aaron is too crook to move far.'

Satisfied that we have considered all options, we decide that I will stay with Aaron and keep the fire built up while Maz backtracks, heading east towards civilization where help can be found.

To the north, Precipitous Bluff rises above the dense forest, crowned by a cloud that looks like a flying saucer. How I wish I could catch a lift home. The cloud changes shape as I watch, stretching and thinning out, allowing me to see the sheer walls of the dominant mountain.

Squatting by the edge of the lagoon to refill water bottles, my eyes wander back to the mountain. The heavily forested lower reaches ascend steeply to the base of the cliffs. Before that there is a sloshy hike alongside the lagoon before you reach the base of the mountain. It's virtually the only way to get up-river, as the vegetation either side of the waterway is almost impenetrable. After heavy rains, negotiating the lagoon becomes more of a challenge, and I have read of hikers wading waist-deep with packs held above their heads. That doesn't sound like much fun. Cavern Camp is about three-quarters of the way along the lagoon's bank and is a sheltered area in which to rest before the push uphill to the summit.

Like so many Tasmanian peaks, Precipitous Bluff is not an undertaking for the faint-hearted. If lucky enough to get to the top in clear weather, the views of the Southern Ocean and mountains inland are by all accounts spectacular. If only I could fly up and over the summit; oh, what a view I would have! I would then veer north-east and make a beeline for Hobart.

It's a bonus having a fresh water supply close to the campground. Run-off from the mountain feeds a creek which flows into the lagoon, and although it's a wet walk to get to drinkable water, it is well worth the effort. Water the colour of tea long-steeped ebbs and flows over my toes as I fill each water bottle in turn. A leaf drifts past in slow motion. More follow; rounded Myrtle leaves shaken loose during the recent storm. Like the leaves, I too have been shaken in recent days and am less confined by expectations that I can control all outcomes. However, unlike the leaves that literally go with the flow – I smile at my unconscious pun – I am increasingly frustrated. It feels like a case of so near and yet so far. I brush leaves from my pants and gather the full water bottles. I know my current mood is in part due to the fact that Maz is leaving camp soon while I'm stuck.

I arrive back at camp and express my frustrations to Maz. She throws an arm around my shoulders. 'You don't think I'm ditching you, do you? We're doubling our chances of rescue this way.' She winks, her grin reassuring.

We have both agreed this plan is giving us the best chance of getting help as quickly as possible. I know we have few other choices given our situation, but logic and emotion are different things.

'Of course, I don't think you're ditching me,' I reply, engulfing Maz in a hug.

'You have been through a lot, Kay,' she whispers close to my ear. 'Trust that you're nearly there and that we'll get Aaron help, and you home, soon. Okay?'

As much as I don't want her to leave, the sooner Maz gets going the more ground she can cover. Days are long at this time of the year and I have no doubt that Maz can move quickly. She should make good progress in a day. With the promise of being reunited again back in Hobart, Maz gives me a thumbs up and strides off to finish her preparations.

Once she's packed up the last of her things, Maz walks over to Aaron and bids him farewell. 'See you back in Hobart, mate.' She hugs Aaron warmly and then hoists her backpack on.

She envelops me in a last hug, squeezing my butt as her lips brush my cheek, and throws her hand in the air in farewell. The sun has barely found its way between the trees. Maz said she has a decent chance of encountering other hikers on the track now that the weather has cleared. If not, she will quick step it to Cockle Creek, a few days walk away. If luck is with us, she will meet someone who has a satellite phone or an EPIRB before then. Maz is an empowering influence and I vow to try and stay positive. With Aaron and I staying here and keeping the fire high, we will not miss fellow hikers travelling from the east or west, and the fire will be visible to any boat or plane in the area – that I will make sure of.

After Maz's departure the camp settles and it seems even the birds don't sing as brightly. Sitting on his haunches, Aaron cradles his cup of coffee and gazes into the distance. He appears calm, his face softer as he takes in his surrounds as if for the first time. His eyes seek the might of Precipitous Bluff, and long he holds the mountains gaze. Although there is no denying his weakness, Aaron stands and reaches out to me, taking my hand in his.

'Come with me to the beach, Kay. I'll have that swim with you now.'

Astonishment renders me speechless. I understand that the ocean is a healing place, however it will require a big effort for Aaron to get over the sand dunes. Convincing me that it is what he wants to do and that he can make it, we set off with some trepidation on my part.

It is a slow trip to get down to the beach as Aaron has to stop several times. Admitting he has not been swimming for many years, Aaron is at first hesitant and then resolute as together we wade through the shallows and out to deeper water. When he is waist-deep, Aaron submerges himself. As he resurfaces, his hair flicks droplets of water that catch sunlight in a halo around his head. He closes his eyes and lies back, face to the sun. Knobby knees break the surface as Aaron spreads his arms wide, floating.

He is not suffering here, the undulating water absorbing his pain and carrying it away. As the lines on his face relax, I turn and swim steady strokes along the line of the foreshore before flipping over to float on the water in turn. It is extraordinary to be here in this vast wilderness, in this raw and unpeopled landscape. Not a road, building, man-made structure or person other than us can be seen, although I am looking forward to that changing soon. It is a privilege to interact with nature in such raw wilderness. Nothing surpasses that feeling for me, except being with the people I love most. Looking up at the big expanse of blue sky above me, I breathe in arguably the clearest air on the planet.

Aaron's white flesh is goosebumped as I coax him from the water. He accepts my ministrations as I rub his thin body briskly with his shirt and pull a jacket around his shoulders. His trust pulls at my heartstrings. Leaning back on the sand, sunshine blankets him. His woollen thermals are aired and dry but Aaron is loath to put them back on.

'Just want to lie in the sun for a bit, feel the sun on my skin.'

A coughing fit ensues. He sits abruptly, head between knees while his body shakes violently. As the spasms subside, I see the fit has taken its toll; sweat beads Aaron's face. I feel helpless watching my friend gasp for air and kick myself that I went along with his crazy suggestion. It takes minutes for his breathing to calm again.

As we recover from our efforts, I gaze at the horizon. Jumping up suddenly, I peer hard into the distance. Yes, there it is – a ship, far out to sea!

Aaron has seen it too, but does not move.

'Do you have any flares?'

He shakes his head.

'I've used all of mine. Damn it!'

I quickly drag more branches towards the fire and upturn the log that Maz and I had sat on last night. I feed the flames, which leap energetically. Logic tells me the ship is a long way out to sea and the chances of it seeing us are thin indeed. Still, I try.

As the flames stretch high, Aaron and I watch as the outline of the vessel melts into the distance with surprising speed, travelling east as engines work hard to get the vessel to the Hobart docks.

Aaron sleeps for hours on the beach while I collect more wood and use rocks to write 'HELP' in large letters on the sand. Rousing him for dinner, I dish up the last of the fish Maz caught. Aaron struggles to eat a few mouthfuls before having to rest. He surprises me with his recovery, sipping a little water and resuming eating. Sometime later he puts down his bowl, having consumed most of what I dished up. I can tell he is pleased to have gotten a meal down. Holding his arms out wide to me, I accept a long hug, Aaron's arms firmly wrapped around me. Feeling his shoulder blades protruding under my palms, I don't want to let go.

'Thank you, Kay,' he says gently, before turning towards his tent, following a path well-lit by the round-bellied moon.

The fire glows, flames dancing lazily in the calm evening. Heaping more branches onto the burning logs, I turn my back to the warmth. Aaron is snoring and sounds more comfortable than he has been for days.

From atop a sand dune, the ocean stares back at me; silent, knowing. Pondering if calm precedes change, I take in the moon's golden glow as it stretches over the ocean, reminding me of the underwater world I explored in my dream last night.

twenty-six
# The dream

The vast bulk of the whale formed a moving mountain in the sea as it rolled to its own rhythm. Partially submerged, I held on tightly, gripping the whale's leathery skin with my knees. My handholds were barnacles and, much as a rock climber does, I gripped the protrusions as if my life depended on it. If the whale propelled itself out of the water, I was a goner. No way could I hold on then.

I held my breath as the whale's fluke beat the water and we dove. Below us a dark ball of fish bounced rapidly away in their underwater playground. Fleeing the whale's baleen-curtained jaws, a fish's tail whacked me in the face as it hightailed away. The whale continued to propel us downwards at a startling speed. A school of silver fish stretched out like a shiny ribbon, then united, grouping tightly as they darted this way and that in an attempt to flee the whale. At close range this was an awesome sight. I forgot to hold my breath as I gasped with the sheer thrill of the chase, the whale and I as one.

The realisation that I could breathe underwater hit me as hard as the fish's tail had, and bubbles of laughter exploded from my mouth. I lay on the whale's back effortlessly as we sped along, flying through the sea; I knew the risk of falling off was a thing of the past and, despite my surprise, the joy to be had in my underwater ride eclipsed all else.

Plunging deeper and deeper into the ocean, surface light diminished and my eyes adjusted to the darker environment. I had the sensation of water flowing over and in me and it was extraordinary, as if I was being washed clean inside and out. The whale started to sing, the pitch varying from a low vibration one moment to a higher trilling sound the next. The sound carried through the water, notes rolling in the wash and flow. Other humpback whales responded to the song, more and more joining in until there was music all around as the whales communicated in their own sing-song language. It was intoxicating, a heady rush of rhythm so beautiful it hurt my ears.

A spectrum of light appeared below me and I found myself momentarily blinded. Magically, the underwater world had lit up, colour exploding and illuminating a myriad of sea life close by. Fish of all colours and sizes danced around us, and from the ocean floor stunning corals and waving sea grasses adorned the vibrant playground. A giant crab lifted up its pincers in greeting and a shark sped by in front of us, sleek as a racing car.

As we reached the seabed, Neptune appeared on his throne in front of me. Sitting atop his rocky seat, the braids of his hair like tentacles, he reached his arms to me and his facial features became clear. It was Aaron in Neptune's guise, greeting me with trident raised in welcome, strong and sure. Seahorses circled his face and mermaids writhed around his sculptured torso. Neptune may have had the head of Aaron but his torso resembled that of the statue of David. He looked commanding and comfortable in his surrounds. One of the mermaids danced before me, the image of Maz, animated and joyful. Her tail brushed me teasingly as she swam past.

I waved to my friends, returning their greetings. The whale seemed to anticipate my reunion with Aaron and brought me closer to my old friend before gently rolling over and depositing me off his back. I felt my own mermaid's tail kick involuntarily, and with delight I joined the mermaid's circle, alongside Maz, dancing around Aaron and moving in time with the music of the whales and movement of the sea.

twenty-seven

# Boot prints

The whirring of helicopter blades buzzes into my dreams and I wake with a hammering heart. I sit upright and the blanket I had wrapped around myself falls forlornly to the sand. Birds shriek as their morning is disrupted by engine noise. It's a helicopter, and it is directly above me! The unmistakable red and yellow Westpac Rescue Helicopter is descending from the sky. Many a time I have seen Westpac choppers on the news and sometimes flying overhead on the way to rescue someone lost or injured in Tasmania's wilderness. Help has arrived in a blaze of sound and colour, and never have I felt such gratitude. Windmilling arms mimic the helicopter blades and I see a face silhouetted in the window of the aircraft.

In the pale dawn light, the outline of my son takes form.

'Matt!' I cry, tears overflowing as I fall to my knees, happiness and shock turning my legs to jelly. I can scarce believe what I am seeing. Matt's grin splits his face as he waves energetically. Joy holds me tight. He is real. This is real. I'm going home.

I spring to my feet as adrenaline courses through me. I run, waving my arms in turn and yahooing. Galloping around the clearing to indicate the boundaries of the makeshift landing pad, I retreat to gaze in awe as the metal bird comes in for landing.

Sand rages at the assault, zipping in all directions and pinging me unmercifully, creating wind that stirs the treetops and causes a pademelon to flee. As the door of the chopper is flung wide, it is unbearably long seconds before I can throw my arms around Matt.

'Mum, you're okay,' he says simply.

Sobbing and laughing simultaneously, I hug him tightly. My eyes are misted over as I hold Matt at arm's length and look at him with relief. I can scarcely believe he is standing in front of me.

'Good spot you've got here, Mum,' he says, grinning. Matt always has a knack of lightening a situation. Thank God he is not in some far-flung part of the world – as an ocean researcher, he works in some remote locations – and is home in Tasmania, though how he hitched a lift on the chopper I don't know and, in this moment, don't care.

I start to apologise for causing such stress when Matt jumps in. 'Mum, it's all good now. Grandad and Grandma and Sasha can't wait to see you.'

I clutch him tightly until I see his eyes fixed on mine and brow furrowed in concern. 'I'm just so overwhelmed to see you, Matt. I'm fine, really.'

He nods and his shoulders drop, a degree of anxiety relieved.

I see the other occupants of the helicopter: a burly male police officer is leaning into the chopper talking to the pilot and a female paramedic is rummaging through an open medical bag on the backseat. Standing respectfully to one side of me is a third man wearing a fluoro jacket that identifies him as a search and rescue officer. His ginger moustache twitches, conveying pleasure that mother and son have been reunited. He strides towards us.

'Pleased to meet you, Kay. I'm Sergeant Gary McDonald from the Police Search and Rescue team,' he says, extending his hand. I throw my arms around him in gratitude, not yet having the words to thank him.

'How are you?' he asks, stepping back and looking at me closely.

'Good now, thank you!'

'That's terrific to hear.'

'Do you know where Sam is?' I ask, my voice shaky. Seeing Matt disembark from the chopper had thrown me off guard and I was distracted in the moment. Now I have asked the question I am terrified of the answer. The paramedic quickly comes to my side and motions for me to sit.

Gary squats. 'He's been through an ordeal but is recovering, Kay, and currently getting well looked after in hospital.'

I start to sob and wrap my arms around my knees, rocking in relief.

Matt sits beside me. Questions tumble out, word over word. 'Is he okay, Matt? Did he send you?'

Gary answers for him. 'Sam is doing as well as can be expected after what he's been through. He is being kept asleep in hospital while his body recovers. He's where he needs to be.'

Relief floods through me. Sam is alive! 'Oh, thank God,' is all I can say. I'm sobbing so hard that tears and snot collide. Matt places his arm around my shoulder. Looking at my son through tears, I see blue eyes that mirror my own. His presence is calming.

Gary is quick to relay the doctor's assurances that Sam's vital signs are improving, despite the obvious blow to the head and hypothermia. I gasp, trying hard to comprehend what Gary is telling me.

'Blow to the head? Hypothermia?' Shaking my head as if to clear it, I try again. 'Where was he found? What happened?

'Mind if we take over for a bit, Matt? You and your mum can catch up shortly.'

'Of course,' Matt says, standing and giving me a quick smile before he moves away. The paramedic introduces herself as

Penny. Her eyes are kind. She is brisk and efficient as she puts a blood pressure cuff on my arm.

Gary reiterates that Sam is being well taken care of, and states that he will fill me in on the details once Aaron joins us.

'Okay, thank you.' I take a deep breath. One thing at a time. 'But how did you find me?'

Gary tells me that Maz encountered a ranger at the next campsite, around ten kilometres on from our current campsite. After relaying our plight, the ranger rang through to Hobart Police on his satellite phone. A rescue team was gathered together and the Westpac Rescue Helicopter was sent south at first light.

After ascertaining that I am in good hands, Gary and the other officer are keen to check on Aaron's welfare. Maz had informed them that a man in very poor health was my companion, awaiting rescue at Prion Beach campsite.

If anyone can sleep through a chopper landing its Aaron, and I tell them so. It's strange he has not yet appeared, nonetheless. Will he be happy to see the rescue chopper and its crew?

A brief conversation ensues and then Gary, who has been talking on the sat phone, briskly sets off towards the campground. The second officer – who introduces himself as Darren – accompanies him.

Penny continues her assessment of me and she asks me how long I have known Aaron, and if he was on the boat with Sam and me.

'Oh no, I met him when a boat dropped me off on shore.'

Seeing the confused look on her face, I add, 'It's a long story.'

'That's alright. I can wait. Let's get you checked out for now.'

Matt is beside me again and I ask about family back home. 'It's alright, Mum. Everyone at home is fine, Sam is okay. We were worried about you. Sasha said to tell you to get home quickly because she wants you to make a celebratory pie with her. Focus on that for now.'

I smile and wipe my eyes, thinking about a pie-making session with Sasha. She has gotten into cooking of late and regularly asks me for family favourite recipes. It is so much fun cooking with her, and her attention to detail and creativity ensure great results. Matt has cleverly diverted my attention to focus on positives.

He is taking in his surrounds with interest. He looks really tired, and guilt courses through me as I realise how harrowing this time period must have been for him, for Sasha, and for Mum and Dad.

The friendly pilot from the police air crew, Ben, stretches out his legs before returning to the chopper. It's challenging to sit still and yet that is what I'm asked to do. As much as I want to get in the air and home as soon as I can, I know that both the police and Penny have my best interests at heart and that I have to trust the process, tedious as it is.

After checking that I have no obvious injuries and am in reasonable health, Penny asks, 'Have you had access to fresh water?'

I assure her that there is water close by and that I have been drinking and eating just fine, under the circumstances. Hence my mouth forms an 'O' of surprise when she tells me I am suffering from mild dehydration.

Asking how I am feeling, I respond, 'I'm fine, thanks. I just want to get moving.'

Penny puts her hand on my back. 'I don't blame you at all. I'm sure we'll be on our way soon. You appear to be in good health, considering what you have been through. Just take it easy for a bit. We'll have you fully hydrated again in no time.'

Penny shakes some hydration salts into a bottle of water and asks me not to move until I have finished drinking the entire bottle. She adds that I need to continue to drink fluids at regular intervals throughout the day and will be further assessed back in Hobart.

'Thanks, Penny,' I say, looking towards the campground and hoping that Aaron, alongside Gary and Darren, will emerge through the trees shortly. 'Is there any chance I can use the sat phone to call home?'

'I don't think so, sorry. You have Matt to chat to though,' Penny responds with a pat on the arm.

'I can tell you what I know about Sam while we wait,' Matt says, sensing my impatience. A fisherman had spied Sam's bright orange life jacket on a rocky shore below East Cloudy Head.

'East Cloudy Head? How did he get there?!'

Matt shrugs in sad resignation. 'Only Sam can answer that, and he's been asleep since they brought him in.'

Wanting to reassure my son, I say what I want to believe. 'Sam is tough, Matt. He'll be okay. He will be talking to us soon enough.'

Matt tells me what he knows about Sam's rescue and injuries. Seeing no signs of life but convinced that there was a body on the rocky and kelp-strewn inlet, the fisherman had put out a Mayday call before going ashore himself. He had held grave fears for Sam. Getting onto the remote – and often treacherous – shore as quickly as he could, he was astounded when he detected that Sam had a faint pulse. He had retrieved a bandage from his first aid box and placed it under the wound on Sam's head, although by that time the bleeding had largely stopped. He then heaped blankets on Sam and continued to reassure him that help was on its way, despite a lack of verbal response. After doing all he physically could, he sat with Sam, radio in hand, talking to him and feeling for his pulse at intervals.

'That's amazing!' I exclaim, resolving to thank him personally at the first possible opportunity.

The fisherman did not leave Sam's side until the police helicopter arrived and winched him to safety from his rocky bed. A nasty gash and swelling on Sam's head, and a few deep cuts and scrapes, were the only external injuries detected. No internal injuries had been discovered. Sam had been slowly warmed and was being monitored in Hobart Hospital. 'He's still in Intensive Care, but I was told he could be moved to a ward soon, and that we'll be able to see him there,' Matt finishes.

I struggle to take it all in yet am desperate to know more, questions overriding each other in my head. I thank Matt and bite back the urge to interrogate him further. There would be plenty of time for questions, and perhaps for a few more answers, later today. He has been through an ordeal too, not knowing where Sam and I were, and no doubt comforting all the family. I will not stress him further.

*Focus on the moment, Kay.*

Gary returns, alone, and sits down with us. Penny gives him the thumbs up. Immediately he asks, 'Kay, do you know where Aaron could be? We can see no sign of him in the camp.'

My eyes widen. 'He must be close by.' Standing, I cup my hands around my mouth. 'Aaron, where are you?'

Gary asks me to sit again. 'Darren is looking around the area, hopefully Aaron will appear soon. He has probably gone to fill his water bottles, or is having a pit stop,' Gary says. Despite his reassurance, I sense his concern. Gary heads back to meet Darren as he emerges from the between the trees. They chat briefly and then Gary calls to me. 'There's no sign of Aaron.'

'Where else would he be?' I ask, startled.

Gary raises an eyebrow. 'I'm hoping you can help us with that, Kay,' he responds kindly. 'Any ideas? Could he have decided to move on?'

Frustrated, I shake my head. 'He's honestly been so sick these past few days. He can't be too far away. I checked in on him just a few hours ago and he was snoring.' Throwing the empty drink bottle aside, I march to the campground with Matt at my side, calling out to Aaron.

A soft light parts the branches of overhead trees and casts a shadowy web across the ground. I wonder if my eyes are deceiving me, for the campground is indeed bare aside from my scant possessions. I stand still, trying to comprehend the empty space where Aaron's tent had been. Ground flattened, the outline of where a tent had stood erect a short time ago is all that remains of my friend's presence. My calls to Aaron become louder as I dash around the campground. Gary, Darren, and Matt are likewise searching the area close by, looking for clues. This is crazy! Aaron is ill and can't have gone far. My belongings, once stored in Aaron's tent, are now piled neatly, resting against the trunk of a tree. There is no note, nor message in the sand; no sign of Aaron that I can detect.

Gary's voice suddenly rings out. 'Over here!'

There, just beyond the tree line and clear as the morning air, are boot prints leading towards New River Lagoon. They are isolated, as sand around the prints has been swept away. Confused, I look back towards where Aaron's tent had stood. We all stand silently, considering the implications of our discovery, before Gary voices the obvious conclusion; Aaron must have been trying to conceal his prints. Snapping off a leafy tree branch from a nearby tree, Gary proceeds to walk backwards, brushing his boot prints away as he backs into the trees.

'That's how he did it. He just missed a few. Do you have any idea why Aaron would conceal his boot prints?' asks Gary.

'No,' I respond, shaking my head in bewilderment.

How could Aaron walk away, particularly given his physical condition; and why would he? Quick to take control, Gary requests that Darren runs back to the helicopter to get Penny, first aid, and day packs. Matt is pensive and looks puzzled, as are we all.

'What were his plans prior to the storm and subsequent events?' Gary asks.

I relay that Aaron had spoken about hiking inland, to Precipitous Bluff, but had not elaborated on his plans. That was before the river crossing, after which his health had deteriorated significantly. 'No way can he walk far in the condition he is in,' I muse. 'Since we made it here in the storm, Aaron has been exhausted and his cough is appalling. Before that, all I know is that he has been suffering from depression and decided to spend some time in wilderness on his own.'

Gary's eyebrow rises. It is a quirk I am getting familiar with. He seems a nice bloke with the right intentions, and I wish I could erase the doubt I can hear in his voice. 'Kay, you said he has an illness. Do you know what it is?'

I tell Gary what I know of Aaron's health concerns and that he has failed to put a name to what ails him medically. 'I think it's a respiratory thing. He coughs all the time and he has a bag load of pills with him.' I think back to the night before and how Aaron had rallied to eat a meal. 'Shit, he did make a big attempt to eat something last night and was acting a bit weird, but I thought it was a sign he was recovering from the river crossing.'

I pause for a moment, contemplating. 'Gary, maybe he actually thinks he can make it to Precipitous Bluff. It seems ludicrous, but Aaron has a strong mind and he's a good bushman. He was out here alone for months before I met him.'

Gary frowns and looks towards the mountain. 'Okay, I'm going to follow these prints, or at least walk a short way in the direction in which I think he will be heading.'

Matt and I follow Gary to the lagoon. There are boot prints at the water's edge. They appear randomly, and some prints are overlaid on top of each other, making the direction they point in hard to decipher. I wonder if that is deliberate. Precipitous Bluff looms above the waterway. I turn to Matt, who takes my hand and gives it a reassuring squeeze. Gary and Penny appear beside us, day packs slung over their shoulders.

Gary hands a radio to Darren, then turns to Matt and me. 'Please stay with Darren while we have a look around.'

I can't believe Aaron has gotten far in his condition. The route to Precipitous Bluff is fraught with challenges even for the fit and prepared. Gary and his team have committed themselves to the rescue of both myself and my sick friend, and they are not going to give up on Aaron easily. Whether they believe Maz and my accounts of Aaron's dire health, I don't know. Certainly, it appears we have been exaggerating, given that Aaron has taken down his tent and walked away unaided.

I shake my head in wonder. I can't believe it either.

We perch on a fallen tree limb on the shore. Matt places sandwiches and tea before me. It is a welcome distraction. I hadn't realised how hungry I am. The sandwiches are a gift from Penny; her lunch I suspect.

'My turn to tell you a good feed is in order, instead of the other way around,' Matt informs me.

'Thanks Matt. I've done okay, considering.'

Matt smiles, 'Yep, you have, Mum,' he concedes with a grin.

I have much more to tell Matt, but that can wait until later. After devouring the sandwiches, Matt produces a battered old cake tin which I instantly recognise as a family hand-me-down. Opening it, he reveals old-fashioned marble cake; my favourite! Savouring the cake, I pay full compliments to the cook.

'Sasha and I couldn't sleep last night after hearing you were okay, so we got together and made a cake.'

Stuffing cake into my mouth, I mumble, 'Thanks, Matt. I can't wait to give Sasha a hug.'

Family is so precious. I have to stay positive. My family are waiting for me back in Hobart. Gary will find Aaron. He will be okay. It will all be okay.

Sated, I lie on the ground, weariness tugging at me. Matt sits beside me, our eyes following the lagoon's trail towards Precipitous Bluff.

'Maz sounds great. Do you want me to fill you in on how she met the ranger?' asks Matt.

'Yes, please!' I reply, happy for the diversion.

She had not arrived at the camp until late evening, limping after twisting her ankle on a boggy stretch of track. Maz is steady on her feet and I can only imagine her injury to have been a result of rushing, or a concealed mudhole, of which there are many on the South Coast Track. The ranger was traveling solo, en route from Cockle Creek. He was walking the South Coast Track, checking trail conditions and what-not. It was a lucky break. Maz had surprised him at the aptly named Surprise Beach campsite, where he was apparently having a swim.

'That'd be right,' I say, shaking my head with a smile.

The ranger will stay with her at the Surprise Beach campsite for another night. The injury is minor, thank goodness. Her plan is to rest for a day or two and then continue on to Cockle Creek. I will be eternally grateful to Maz and look forward to giving her a hug of appreciation at the earliest opportunity.

'Your grandma believes that if we think positively, outcomes are more likely to be positive. I know you feel like that, too. I've been trying so hard to stay positive. It has helped. It hasn't been easy though,' I say, turning to Matt.

Matt nods. 'Yes, Grandma has been trying to keep everybody's spirits up. I know she will be very happy to see you home, though.'

He is close to his grandma and has some similar traits. Both are gentle, warm, and loving individuals who have that rare ability to put others' needs before their own. They also have firm convictions and are not easily swayed.

I am deeply grateful. Matt is beside me. Soon I will see Sam and family again. My belly is full. However, I have a knot of fear in my stomach regarding Aaron's wellbeing. It seems he has chosen to continue on his own journey, doing things his way and putting faith in the healing powers of nature. I am afraid for him and astounded by his actions, yes, but deep down I also feel a great respect for him. Silently, I send out a prayer for my friend. In the short time I have known him, I have come to understand that peace is what he craves beyond all else, and my hope is that he finds it.

twenty-eight
# A clue

Dappled sunlight sprays my bare legs and sends shadows skipping across my eyelids. Surprised to have fallen asleep, I rub my eyes. I breathe a sigh of relief on seeing Matt beside me, hat over his face as he lies back against the log. The thought of sitting down at a dinner table with Mum, Dad, Sasha, Matt, and Sam fills me with sudden joy. I hear voices and turn my head towards the lagoon.

'They're on their way back, Matt!' I exclaim.

He jumps and I realise I have startled him into wakefulness.

'You two had a good bit of shut-eye,' Darren comments, walking up to us from a nearby tree against which he had been leaning. He has a deep voice and is a big man who looks as strong as an ox, as Dad would say.

'Have you heard any news yet?' I ask.

'They radioed me about thirty minutes ago and said they were on their way back. It looks like we'll get an update soon enough,' he adds as Gary and Penny appear, and make their way towards us.

Gary starts talking as soon as he is close enough for us to hear him. 'The boot prints disappear a short way up the path, where scrub encroaches on the waterline. We couldn't go any further without having a wade upstream.'

'I don't reckon that Aaron crossed to the other side of the lagoon. It's too dangerous, given its swollen state,' comments Penny.

'It looks like Aaron may have done what you suggested, Kay, and is sticking to the trail that heads towards Precipitous Bluff on this side of the lagoon.'

Gary and Penny had backtracked, scouring the scrub close to the shoreline but finding nothing to indicate that Aaron had detoured away from the water. I recall that a friend had summited the mountain from the other side a few years ago, and had then continued south to Prion Beach. When speaking of his hike he had told me that he had waded in thongs for two hours on the last part of his journey. It had been hot weather when he did it and there had been little rain for months, meaning that the lagoon depth was about as low as it gets. Although he had been very fit at the time, he did question his choice of footwear on the water route, saying it had been a particularly slow and slippery slog. If the hike is challenging in dry weather, how much more so would it be after big rains?

'He has good boots,' I declare, trying to find a positive and wanting badly to believe Aaron will succeed in the mission he is on, whatever that may be.

'I hope Aaron is in better shape than you believe, Kay,' Gary says. 'As you said, he has a strong mind and good boots. Maybe his meds, rest, and your ministrations have helped him more than you know. I'm not giving up on him, but we do have to get you back to Hobart before dark, okay?'

Gary looks skywards, pointing to the building clouds. Apologetic but nonetheless firm, he states that we will prepare to fly back to Hobart as quickly as can. Gary is not going to take chances.

'But what about Aaron – we can't just leave him,' I state.

'We'll have to get ground search and rescue into the area. An organised foot party is the best way of doing a thorough search,' replies Gary. 'Aaron has made a choice, and, as you said, he's a skilled bushman. I'm sorry I can't do more at this stage,' he adds, seeing my dismay.

'Let's get you back to Hobart, to Sam,' Penny's says with a reassuring smile.

With Penny's words as incentive, it takes little time to get my gear ready for my departure. I look around and realise I am on my own, momentarily. I take the opportunity and jog up a sand dune to have a final look around from a higher vantage point. Turning slowly, I take in my surroundings, searching in vain hope for a sign of some sort from Aaron.

'Let's go, Kay,' calls Gary from behind me.

'Just give me a moment and I'll be there.'

Looking out across the sea, I gaze at the horizon where sky and ocean are seemingly divided by intensity of colour only. The clarity of air and water in Tasmania is a drawcard for many, yet still lines can be indistinguishable, a trick of lighting causing an obscuring of definitions. I want to get back to Hobart, desperately, but feel as if I am deserting Aaron. The blurring of lines between the responsibility I feel for another and my own needs is unsettling. Making my way to the helicopter, I look skywards to where a sea eagle dips low, gliding north. The eagle's wings beat the air with steady insistence, picking up speed as it soars higher towards the mountain. If only I could glide on eagle's wings. It would give me some peace to see a man trekking through the bush, cigarette drooping from his lips and in the environment that he is most comfortable in. I sense that for Aaron there is no turning back; he is moving forward towards his own destiny. That I have not been able to say goodbye makes my heart ache.

Gary tries to allay my fears as he is closing the door of the helicopter, after ensuring I am seated. 'A ground search and rescue party will be organised for tomorrow, as long as the weather holds,' he tells me.

I look up at the grey clouds. Matt gives me a quick hug. 'It sounds like Aaron is a man who knows his own mind, Mum.'

Matt's words are exactly what I need to hear, and mirror my own thoughts. It's time to go home. I can do no more here.

Ben issues instructions to us as he is lifting the helicopter up, nose rotating to point towards the lagoon. Up, up, we rise, disturbing a flock of low flying waterbirds that divide and split into two separate formations. Shockwaves from the helicopter cause a mini tsunami on the lagoon, and insects crash land in the shrubbery as the chopper blades whip through the air. A currawong bursts through the branches of a tree, alarmed enough to drop a treasured find from its beak.

'Wait!' I call through my mouthpiece.

The bird had been carrying a bag which had burst on impact with the ground. Rubbish is blowing upwards in the chopper's wake, lighter items cartwheeling this way and that. A paper wrapper flattens against a tree trunk before dancing free to take flight.

We are all straining to see out the windows of the helicopter. Gary speaks briefly to Ben, who nods before turning the helicopter and flying low over the lagoon and surrounding bush. Ben now follows the lagoon's path inland.

'Just a quick look-see,' Ben tells us through his microphone.

All eyes are firmly fixed on what is below.

The scrub on either side of the lagoon is so thick it looks to be impenetrable from our vantage point. Precipitous Bluff rises up dramatically and Matt and I stare, transfixed by the mountain's growing presence. Ben follows the course of the lagoon northwards, then cuts back and forth across the waterway, extending the search area to encompass nearby bush. I gape in awe at the jagged flanks of the mountain as we ascend to higher altitudes.

'Where is he? There's no way could Aaron get up there!' I exclaim.

Matt nods. Everything I have told him indicates how remote that possibility is. Our search yields no further sign of Aaron's progress. Gary turns from his position in the front seat and points to the darkening sky.

'Time's up – we need to stay ahead of the weather. We'll get back out here as quickly as possible, that you can be sure of.'

That bag of rubbish has confirmed – in my mind – my theory on Aaron's movements. 'Aaron always ties his rubbish bag to the front of his pack. His bag might have snagged on something and been ripped from his backpack.'

Gary nods in agreement. The bird could have then claimed it, scattering its contents. I no longer have any doubt about the direction Aaron has pursued.

As the helicopter turns and dips back down towards the coastline, I feel Matt's hand cover mine. We fly over the highest peppermint gums and, like giants awakening, they shudder and shake, indignant to be roused from slumber. Leaves whirl through the air, fanning out to spin wildly before settling on the water below. There, the leaves are caught in eddies created by the helicopter's updraft, alighting on ripples which spread out into the ocean in ever widening arcs. Prion Beach is quickly camouflaged, engulfed by the protective arms of coastal vegetation. As the nose of the helicopter points east, I send out a silent blessing for Aaron's boots to carry him safely to his destination.

Matt gives me a thumbs up as the chopper buzzes onwards. 'Home, Mum. Sasha is waiting with Grandma and Grandad,' he tells me, eyes smiling.

My family will have a pot of tea at the ready, awaiting news of my adventures and with a million questions, and they will be keen to fill me in on all I have missed at home. It is a good thought.

I finally allow myself to think more about Sam. I have felt him throughout my ordeal. I am surprised when I turn and he is not physically beside me. Focusing on getting through the moment is what Sam has taught me. The certainty that Sam will recover when I am there by his side is strong. I can finally rejoice in the reality of my homecoming.

Squeezing my eyes tightly closed, I conjure up an image of Sam on the last day I saw him; bronzed from the sun, feet planted wide on the deck of *Mulwala*. My heart had missed a beat as he turned to me with a twinkle in his eyes, and that cheeky grin I know so well.

twenty-nine
# Homeward bound

As I gaze out the chopper window at the wilderness below, I admire the coastline and mountains that retreat in seemingly never-ending folds. I reflect on how nature has provided for me, guided me, and given me the tools to survive. I have changed irrevocably in ways I cannot yet fully fathom. I know myself better for all that has passed, and am certain of the things I want in my life. I have more self-belief, and have been challenged and conquered fears. I can survive on my own – even in extreme conditions, with a bit of luck thrown in – but prefer the company of others; those who I care about and who care about me in turn.

There is so much to talk to Sam about. I see my face reflected in the window and close my eyes, replacing my image with Sam's. His face is creased by weather and wind, his eyes are warm and smile at the ready. A passion for the environment first drew us together, and I plan to inspire Sam to heal by talking about getting back out into the wilds of Tasmania. I will allow no room in my head to believe anything other than that we have many adventures together yet to be played out.

I focus on my surroundings in hope that I can control the rollercoaster of emotions that my homecoming threatens to unleash. Dense vegetation and craggy peaks dominate the land mass beyond the coastline. White sand beaches and bays sparkle on land's periphery, devoid of footprints; the jewels of the south. The division between land and sea, safety and peril, appears clear from this height. Our sense of wellbeing can be deceptive.

I have flown along this coastline with Sam en route to Melaleuca to walk the South Coast Track. Although I had read prior that the walk is considered one of the most remote wilderness walks in the world, I had been unprepared for the reality of that. Over the eight days it took us to complete the hike, the raw beauty of the landscape buoyed Sam and I. Our bond had deepened through shared circumstance. Trust and reliance on each other were critical to our enjoyment in what can be an inhospitable environment. Sam and I worked together as a tight unit as we traversed from Melaleuca to Cox Bight, around bluffs and headlands, along wild stretches of pristine coastline, and across the Ironbound Range, to finally emerge from the bush at Cockle Creek.

The tiny hamlet of Cockle Creek marks the edge of the Southwest National Park and is the most southerly town in Australia. On nearing the settlement, we had encountered day trippers who had looked alien to us in their clean attire; as we no doubt did to them, muddied and dishevelled as we were. Both parties had detoured around each other.

I grimace as I look down at myself, reflecting that I don't look much different now to what I did then. I comment to Matt that I badly need a shower.

'Sam will just be glad to see you, Mum,' he says, and I hug him. He pinches his nose and makes a face. We both laugh.

The button grass plains we are flying over are a vast expanse of mudflats. They lie in wait, like hungry monsters, behind towering headlands and alluring beaches and bays. It is easy to reflect on how hiking the South Coast Track with Sam had prepared me well for the struggle to survive in wilderness. Hard times inevitably bring rewards; the trick is hanging in there and persevering. I have finetuned that art in recent times, for sure.

Suddenly, a Shy Albatross appears, gliding parallel to the helicopter high above the rocky headland of Surprise Beach campsite.

'Albatross,' I shout through my microphone, pointing.

The helicopter and bird momentarily fly side by side. Circling once, twice, the albatross then changes direction to fly south, eyes seeking as she turns her head to look directly at me.

*May you fly long and strong, my friend.*

I silently rejoice in my belief that Eva has survived and is flying free.

The chopper dips and descends slightly, before levelling out above the base of the rocky incline that leads upwards to Surprise Beach campsite. Figures appear on the beach below and are waving at us. There's Maz, waving energetically. What a ball of energy she is.

'I'm here!' I shout.

Of course, she can't hear me, but I can't stop myself. Matt laughs as Gary turns and smiles, giving me a thumbs up. Ben circles above the small group on the beach as we wave in turn. Maz ditches her backpack and throws her hat in the air, as wind stirred up by the chopper's wings picks up her ponytail and whips it across her face. Waving in turn, I nearly knock Matt in the face.

'Maz helped Aaron and me so much,' I say to Matt. 'I can't wait to introduce you.'

'I'm looking forward to meeting her,' Matt responds, his eyes twinkling.

On and over distinctive South Cape Range we fly, fluted cliffs marking the western face of the impressive range. Recalling scary river crossings – all too familiar on this section of the track – I vividly remember Sam reaching out to me as

I fought to negotiate my way through waist-deep water. He was my hero on that epic hike, and it was only then that I had realised I was in love with my best friend. Sam is a loveable type of guy with a big heart. As my partner, he is caring and supportive and there is rarely a day that he fails to make me laugh. Even when he is annoying me to no end, his ability to turn things around with humour generally wins me over. Sam and I had sloshed through endless mud and water before we saw South East Cape jutting out like an exclamation mark, reminding us to turn inland.

Veering away from the most southerly point of Tasmania (and of Australia) I point out a familiar landmark to Matt, directly below our flight path. 'There's Lion Rock.'

It casts a long shadow below us with head held high, a warning to those who dare to venture south beyond her flanks. Waves crash up against the cape as we buzz over the rocks, turning our backs to the wind, bound for Hobart. To the west, clouds race each other.

Matt has repeatedly assured me that the doctors at the Royal Hobart Hospital are optimistic Sam will recover fully. His head scans are clear. I have played out different scenarios in my mind as to what happened to Sam. I believe he must have fallen overboard and been distanced from the yacht within minutes, as the engine propelled *Mulwala* forward. I am grateful that Sam is a stickler for boating protocol and always wears a life jacket when sailing, even though it restricts swimming ability.

I think he must have sustained the knock to his head as he tumbled through surf onto a rocky shore. It's a miracle he is alive. A clairvoyant once told me I had a guardian angel on my shoulder. Initial scepticism had given rise to intrigue and a sense of comfort. It seems Sam is being watched over. Never once, since I woke up on *Mulwala* alone, have I given up on my belief that Sam is alive; nor that Sam would give up on me.

Matt is pointing out Bruny Island. He is animated, and I realise that he has not flown over this part of the world before. Pushing aside my thoughts, I press my nose up against the glass pane. Views of Bruny and the channel emerge as we fly north up the coast. East Cloudy Head juts seawards below Mount Bruny, a talisman, beyond which are the protective waters of Cloudy Bay. From our vantage point, the three-kilometre white sand beach under us looks stunning. Matt gives me a thumbs up, pointing out the bay that he, Sam, and I had sailed to a few summers ago. Happy memories. It was these memories that had given rise to Sam's and my holiday plans.

'I'm coming, Sam,' I whisper, leaning my head back against the seat and taking a deep breath. I am nearly home.

thirty
# River

To the west, hungry clouds are rapidly consuming the sun. Looking east through the front window of the helicopter, the sky is blue and clear. If I had not heard Gary's forecast or looked behind to the dark clouds, I could well be deceived by the weather gods. As the helicopter's shadow flits past, I see sunlight reflected off a small motorboat tied to the jetty at Partridge Island. It feels like an eon of time has elapsed since Sam and I departed the tiny island aboard *Mulwala*. The channel looks benign today, as it had been then. We had sat on deck with drinks in hand as dusk settled around us like a soft blanket.

'Look at those guys,' Matt exclaims, pointing excitedly.

Seals roll lazily in the water, just outside of the yellow boundary markers of a fish farm below. Flying over the familiar landmarks of the D'Entrecasteaux Channel, the sense of coming home is acute. From Cockle Creek to Hobart, small communities with quaint names like Flowerpot and Snug are strung along the coast like a bower bird's treasures. The Bruny Island ferry is on route back to Kettering from the island, a white wake cutting the water cleanly behind it.

Gary leans forward to have a word with Ben. Not being privy to their discourse, I focus my attention on the waterway below. Kingston Beach comes into view. It's a popular place for pooches. Below, dogs run this way and that, sniffing and circling each other. Several bound through the waves to retrieve sticks or balls flung by their owners. The bulk of kunanyi/Mount Wellington rises in the foreground, indomitable, looming protectively over Hobart city and local waterways.

'Mum, we're nearly there.'

Indeed, we are.

Below us, houses are dotted between trees and headlands, clustered more closely together the nearer we get to Hobart. Boats on moorings add decoration to the River Derwent, and appear like baubles strung at intervals along the shoreline. As the helicopter steadily descends, swimmers in the water at Long Beach came into view; a few look up at us and wave. Sandy Bay boasts the most well-known beach in Hobart and has the most impressive real estate. There is Australia's oldest casino, standing proud yet always looking a little out of place – the tall girl at the party.

Neat rows of yachts and motorboats are lined up behind the break wall of the Derwent Sailing Squadron, and alongside is the fancier Royal Yacht Club of Tasmania. On returning home after a weekend of sailing with Sam, the sight of yacht masts looming above the marinas always feels welcoming, as they do today. How quickly we have reached home! Heart in mouth, I dig my nails into my palms as the Tasman Bridge, the gateway from Hobart to the eastern shore, comes fully into view.

Sullivans Cove opens up before us as the helicopter continues its steady descent. It is here that Sydney to Hobart boats tie up after finishing the famed race, fatigued crews disorientated and often overwhelmed by the cheering crowds lining the wharfs. A welcome respite to weary sailors, Sullivans Cove tucks neatly into the city's waterfront.

It was from here that Sam and I had departed the city aboard *Mulwala*, sailing into our holiday with welcome relief, a busy summer of work behind us. I remember Sam cracking jokes as we had left the city behind, seeing his shoulders finally relax, feeling mine do likewise. The thought of sunshine, laying back on deck – me with a book and Sam with his fishing line – had enticed us into a feeling of wellbeing. We had not been complacent; that was against Sam's careful nature and my need to be organised, but we had been rushed in our preparations, keen to get going. I frown, remembering.

The blades of the helicopter whip around, sending shivers across the verdant green of the Domain as we prepare to land. Camera crews and reporters await us, and I feel momentary panic. I want to be at Sam's side as quickly as I can. Penny explains that an ambulance will meet us when we land. It is protocol that I undergo a few more routine medical checks once at the hospital, before being given the all clear to see Sam.

'Matt, you can travel with your mum in the ambulance,' she adds kindly, giving me a reassuring smile. I smile weakly in turn.

After we have landed, the doors of the chopper are pulled open and hands reach out to me. I lean back instinctively, flustered by the crowd of people and the attention. Gary puts a coat around me and ushers Matt and I in the direction of the ambulance, Penny right alongside us. If an ambulance is the quickest way out of here then I am happy for the ride.

'What happened to your yacht?' asks a reporter who has positioned himself at the door of the ambulance.

'How did you and Sam get separated?' another asks.

Gary asks the reporters to give me some space.

'Only answer if you want to, Kay.'

'I woke up aboard our yacht, alone. Sam wasn't on the boat,' I respond, turning to the media with a tremor in my voice. Reporters jostle for position. '*Mulwala* sank and I was lucky to make it to land.' I take a trembling breath and continue. 'I am grateful to be alive and thankful to all who helped in the rescue of both Sam and I.' I'm choking back tears and, frustrated, I turn away from the reporters.

Declining to answer any further questions, I offer no protest when Penny asks me to step into the ambulance. I'm shaking, and feel cold and clammy. It's a relief to have the doors closed behind me.

thirty-one
# Hobart

My eyes seek the river through the windows of the ambulance as we drive down the hill into the heart of Hobart. An afternoon sea breeze plays with the water, kicking up white tufts, plucking and teasing.

Hobart is a pretty city. Stretching out below the mountain, the river provides a natural boundary. Buildings vie for space but are careful not to crowd. An afternoon yacht race is taking place in what I guess to be a breeze of around fifteen knots, creating good sailing conditions. Sails stretch, full bellied as the boats fly along, bows pointed towards the Tasman Bridge. Soon they will round the marker, tack back into the wind. Looking at the water is distracting and helps me to relax, momentarily at least. Penny gives my hand a little squeeze as she tucks a comforting blanket around me.

Knowing I will soon be by Sam's side, my heart rate quickens. I don't want to see him suffering, and if he is, I'm afraid that all the emotions that are vying for space within me will erupt.

*God, please let him be doing better.*

It is as if the busyness of Hobart and closeness to loved ones has heightened all of what I am feeling and my thoughts spin this way and that, as capricious as the River Derwent's moods.

While Gary has acknowledged that my priority is to see Sam, he has cautioned me to be patient. At some stage police would need my assistance; it is inevitable that reports be filed and essential for police to have all the information I can give to them. There is much curiosity as to the disappearance of *Mulwala*, and to subsequent events. That there is a third person missing, when Sam and I are now accounted for, adds intrigue to a story that already has puzzling undertones. I will use time with the police to ask a few questions myself and am determined to take the opportunity to stress Aaron's ill health.

I am overwhelmed by all I see as I look out the window of the ambulance; people, cars, the city itself. The hospital comes into view. I take a deep breath as my stomach flip-flops with anticipation. The need to see Sam – to just lay eyes on him – is intense. Maybe my heart will stop beating so fast then.

*I can't lose it now.*

As the doors of the emergency department slide open, Penny and Matt stay alongside the wheelchair I have been transferred to.

'Why is it that hospitals always want us in wheelchairs?' I ask Penny, adding, 'I want to run!'

Penny shrugs but with a wink responds, 'To stop people running, maybe?'

Nurses bustle past us. Anxious faces barely glance at me as people wait to be attended to or give comfort to the distressed. I am promptly ushered into a closed cubicle after a brief goodbye to Penny. Matt goes to phone Sasha, who will pass on news to family. A plain-clothed policeman waits outside the cubicle. The police want to interview me once a doctor has given clearance for them to do so. What choice do I have other than to accept the process?

*Bloody bureaucracy.*

Darkness descends sometime during the hours it has taken for my medical checks to be completed, treatment given – a few scrapes patched up and a mild sedative prescribed, should

I require it – and a police interview conducted in order to fill out appropriate forms. I refuse a drip for hydration and instead drink yet another bottle of water, have a quick clean-up, and eat some soggy tomato sandwiches that I struggle not to choke on. I am given a referral to see a psychologist. Although tedious, the medical report concluded I am in good general health and that mood aberrations noted – anxiety, high and low mood swings – are consistent with trauma. Rest is advised.

After what seems like an eternity, Matt and I, accompanied by a member of medical staff, are on our way to the Intensive Care Unit. As night closes in on Hobart city, a hush penetrates the hospital walls. The polished corridors echo our footsteps. A door to a small hospital chapel stands open, revealing an old man sitting alone, finding comfort in his faith.

Squaring my shoulders, I will my hammering heart to quieten and face the doors of the Intensive Care Unit. Staff have been warned of our arrival. Matt and I are met by a doctor, who addresses us; clinical and to the point.

'Sam's vital signs are good, and while he has regained consciousness, he is slow to respond and is sleeping a lot. That's to be expected. As of this morning, Sam is breathing on his own. Tests have indicated no sign of any long-term brain damage, which is very good news. However, his traumatic brain injury will need monitoring over the months to come. He will be moved from Intensive Care to a ward within the next twenty-four hours, all going well. He has suffered significant trauma and will require some therapy and time to heal after his ordeal.'

The doctor cautions that while his physical state is much improved, rest is a key priority. Sam's mental scars will take longer to heal.

*For both of us.*

'You do expect Sam to recover fully, though?' I ask.

'I certainly believe so,' the doctor tells me, his tone softening.

I give Matt a quick but joyful hug.

'Great news, Mum,'

A nurse, who introduces herself as Margie, turns to Matt.

'Unfortunately, only your mum can visit Sam at this time, Matt. Once Sam is moved to a ward, which he will be shortly we hope, you'll be able to visit him.'

Margie says she will show me to Sam's bedside. I farewell Matt briefly before Margie leads me through the doors of the ICU. Margie is of a similar age to me and has brown hair flecked with grey, pulled back in a loose ponytail. She has warm eyes. She reaches out and lightly places her hand on my arm.

'He will be do better for you being here,' she declares, her voice tender.

I am glad it is she who is caring for Sam. Margie pauses as the doors of the ICU close behind us. 'Just give me a moment to check Sam's vitals,' she requests.

I can't move, so shocked am I to finally see Sam in the flesh. He appears to be asleep. Margie checks a monitor, straitens his pillows, then murmurs to him. I hear her say my name but nothing more. Margie waves me forward. A sob catches in my throat as I reach Sam's bed. Margie steps discreetly aside as I place a light kiss on Sam's lips.

'Sam, I'm here.'

I rest my forehead on Sam's inert hand. Threading my own hand under his, tears slide between our fingers and dampen the bed covers. I sob uncontrollably. Margie steps forward again, rubbing my back in light circular sweeps, reassuring me.

'Drowsiness is normal after a head trauma, and Sam has recently been given medication for pain which has sent him back to sleep, unfortunately.'

I nod dumbly as Margie once more retreats.

Moments pass as I try to control my crying. I raise my head to gaze at Sam's face. His chest rises and falls ever so lightly. He appears smaller than I remember, lying in this neatly made bed. Sam would approve; he likes neat beds. I'm the messy one. In so many ways we help balance each other. A small smile tugs at my mouth as, with my hand holding his, I rub my eyes and take in all of him. He has lost weight, but he's here in front of me and he's real and he's breathing.

'Sam, it's Kay. I'm here,' I whisper close to his ear.

His eyes stay closed and he snores in that way Sam does when he is deep in sleep, more like an irregular whistle than a snore. This familiarity helps to restore equilibrium within me. As if a heavy cloak has been lifted from my shoulders, I collapse onto the chair beside the bed.

Sam's head has been shaven and a large dressing is held in place with a stretch bandage. I observe his pallor, sunken cheeks, and stubble. Regardless, he is my Sam and I love every whisker.

'Sam, wake up. I'm here,' I whisper again, as I stroke his hand.

Sam's hands are those of a man used to physical labours, however, at present they feel like coarse sandpaper, as if he has scraped them along the ocean floor. One shoulder is badly bruised, the white sheet in stark contrast to the deep purple. I stand and lean over him, lightly kissing his eyelids, his cheeks. As my lips touch Sam, I feel a flutter of movement. I jerk back and stare intently at him. A slight frown draws his eyebrows closer together and his eyelids flutter in a ripple of movement.

Margie is checking the chart of a patient in a nearby bed and glances my way. She hastens over. 'Sam is not fully aware yet. That does not mean he can't hear and feel you, Kay, he may just be doing so through a bit of a fog. He is exhausted and it may take a few more days for him to be alert and to have normal responses. Give him a little longer – his body is telling him to rest.' She gives me a warm smile. 'Be patient. Sit with him for a bit and I will come back in fifteen minutes or so.'

Sam's heart is beating and I needed to see that to believe it, I now realise. Pulling the chair closer to the bed, I graze my lips over his knuckles. The weight of Sam's hand on mine is both familiar and comforting.

Sinking back down onto the chair, I prepare to wait.

thirty-two
# Sam

A feather-light kiss arouses me and blood courses through my veins. The warmth creates tendrils of light that seek to penetrate the dense fogginess that surrounds me. I try to surface, to respond to Kay's calls just like before; before this bed, before the sea claimed me. My eyelids are weighted down. Images flash like a school of colourful fish, merging, hard to decipher. If I can go back, understand what has led me here, maybe then I can reach Kay. I allow myself to sink, deeper and deeper.

I recall swimming and the effort required to keep going. Cold penetrated, making movement difficult and my chest heavy, as if my lungs were solidifying. Water rushed past, then over me. My legs were leaden and no matter how much I willed them to keep kicking, they started to sink of their own volition. Waves rose and fell, rolling, pushing me along.

Soft lips brush over my knuckles, prodding my subconscious. I am looking down on myself as I drift in a bed on the ocean, and know that past and present have collided. I'm dreaming, and although I know I am in a bed, I can feel the ocean pulling me. I want to reach out to Kay yet fear drowning. It's so hard to fight the pull downwards into the dark and watery depths. My bed disappears and I'm sinking.

Picking up my arms and willing my legs to kick, I swim on in my dreaming state, the ocean moving ceaselessly under me and dictating direction. *Mulwala* is now a long way away, bobbing like a cork to God-knows-where. And so it is that the sea picks me up and carries me far away from *Mulwala*.

Disappearing intermittently in the swell, the yacht's lights became pinpricks on the horizon. It is better not to fight the sea; that I know. I can finally see the outline of land. I let my arms fall. They're too heavy to hold up anymore. A bright light flashes ahead of me periodically, as waves surrender to troughs. The dark shape of land is slowly reeling me in. It is my only hope.

I am not scared, strangely. Not even pissed off, as I had been when first flung from *Mulwala*. Then I had cursed till I was hoarse.

My hands are losing feeling. I attempt to flex my uncooperative fingers, making out their shape in the darkness. I try to hug my knees into my chest and curl around my core in order to generate some body warmth. Quickly tiring, I only manage to bend my knees slightly before I succumb once more to the rhythm of the sea and drift. Saving what little energy I have left.

I can see myself clearly now, as if I'm somehow high above my body, looking down. I'm a small dot in a big ocean, being swept along at the sea's bidding. I will be washed to shore; that is inevitable. There is more danger where the ocean meets land, reef, and rocks. I need to be prepared so that I can use the waves close to shore to my advantage. As soon as I feel the tug of land, know that shoreline is close, I need to start swimming.

It is hard to focus; my mind keeps wandering and I sense I am blacking out regularly. Stirring myself, I feel for my life jacket, relieved to find it secure on my torso. A light attached to the jacket is flashing in the water beside me. Clumsily picking up the whistle – likewise attached to the jacket – I attempt to blow on it, spluttering as water catches in my throat. I manage

thirty-three
# Family

A furrow forms on Sam's brow and I smooth it gently with my fingertip.

'What are you dreaming about, Sam?'

I place my lips lightly on his, hoping he can feel me; hoping he can hear me.

Maz may have been able to call through to Hobart by now from a service area. She has Matt's and Sasha's numbers. Her voice would be a balm for the soul. Dad and Mum will have been on the phone wanting updates; wanting to see me. Sasha would have called them as soon as Matt let her know we were back in Hobart. Phone calls are not allowed in the Intensive Care Unit but I long to hear the voices of my family, and to check in with Maz.

Matt had assured me Sasha was good, just hanging out to see me. I know exactly how she is feeling; seeing someone in the flesh makes things real. It's not fair not to call her, as she will be wanting to hear the sound of her mum's voice – as I do hers. I close my eyes and hear Sasha's voice. I'm crying now, crying rivers of tears. My daughter's voice is strong.

Turning back to Sam, I trace his fingers with my own, willing movement no matter how small. I lower my forehead to his upturned hand as weariness tugs at me unmercifully. My head is cradled in this position. I feel his fingers flex ever so slightly.

Kissing his palm, I wait for a response just to be sure. But I am. A ripple of joy runs through my body, extending all the way to my toes.

'Time for a break, Kay,' states Margie, a hand on my shoulder.

'He moved,' I tell her, a tremor in my voice. 'I think he's dreaming,' I add in wonder.

Margie nods but is insistent on getting me to the door and out into a waiting area. She makes me a cup of tea, declaring visitors are on their way to meet me – my son and daughter, no less.

I pace the floor with my mug of tea, watching the hallway. Yes, there they are! Sasha is striding ahead, looking stylish as always, her liquid brown hair catching the light as it flicks from side to side, like a rain-washed river. I am so proud of this girl of mine; what a woman she has become. Confident, successful, with a sharp wit and lively humour. Matt and she get along very well; she is intense – like her mum – and he has a more mellow personality. They balance each other and theirs is a strong sibling relationship.

'Mum,' she calls out, moving more quickly now. Matt stands back, smile plastered wide as Sasha reaches me and we fall into each other's arms. Oh, how good it feels to hug my daughter! Sasha holds me tightly, when normally her hugs are brief and perfunctory as she's always rushing. She is happy to see me. Tears fall afresh and we are both laughing and crying and asking questions at the same time.

'Mum, can you *please* stay put for a while now?' she asks in mock exasperation.

'I am not planning any big adventures again for quite a while,' I reply.

Sasha has long wanted me to be at home more, my adventurous nature taking me away regularly. Matt has the same adventurous streak but is more of a daredevil than I, which worries both his mum and his sister. We must all live our own lives, but I am in full agreement with Sasha that home is the best place in the world, as long as loved ones are not too far away.

Matt joins us in a corner of the waiting area as tea and biscuits miraculously appear from a tea trolley. Sasha and Matt banter as usual, and I look on with a full heart. Home. Family. Now all we need is for Sam to get well and join us. She wants to know how I survived when *Mulwala* did not, what happened to Sam, and how the heck I ended up on Pedra Branca. Reasonable questions.

'Grandma and Grandad have been really worried, Mum,' Sasha informs me. 'I can tell Grandad isn't coping well – he's been really grumpy.'

Matt nods. 'Grandma kept saying you would be okay.'

*Good on you, Mum.* She has always held great faith in my abilities to fend well for myself (although, in more recent times, she has admitted that a show of outward faith helps her inward confidence).

'Are they both okay?' I ask.

Despite having had excellent health most of their lives, both are in their seventies now. Mum had a health scare a few years back, finding a lump on her breast. Although it was found to be benign, it scared me and does still. I had gone to the doctor with her and had felt the lump myself. It had been hard and looked wrong. The doctor assured us that it was an enlarged lymph node and the tests he ordered backed this up. Still, I am relieved when each check-up comes back clear. I have always had a special bond with my mother.

I realise how much I need to hear my mum's voice, and how I take it for granted that she will always be there. I'll ring her and Dad – whose banter I miss almost as much as Mum's hugs – as soon as I can.

'Grandad is eating too many chocolate bars,' says Sasha, interrupting my thoughts. 'Me too,' she adds as an afterthought. She laughs as she whips a block of chocolate out of her bag and proceeds to break it up, handing Matt and I generous portions.

Margie appears, beckoning us forward with the words we have longed to hear.

'He's awake!'

thirty-four
# Into the wild

A night owl is on watch. There is a hollow tree close to my resting place and, as I have not moved for many hours, I suspect the Southern Boobook has come to rest in the tree. Its soft wings barely cause a disturbance. I am highly attuned to sound, my senses alert, as if I have become a creature of the environment. Aaron, the man, is a distant part of me now. There are worst fates.

I will rest for a while longer to conserve what energy I have left. It will take all of my remaining strength to get to my destination. I have no regrets. My mind is free to wander. My heart is also freed – at last – to savour the sounds, smells, and feel of the bush. To savour my memories. A short time ago a sun shower quenched my thirst. As I tilted my head up, mouth open to catch the moisture, water trickled under my coat hood. It ran down my back in a little stream. Not that it bothered me.

I was reminded of my swim with Kay. What a glorious gift that was. I hadn't had a swim for many years prior. The need to immerse myself in the sea had been overwhelming, and the sensation of moving through water that so perfectly mirrored the blue sky something special. It made it easy to imagine moving through one medium and into another. I have felt cleansed ever since, body, mind, and spirit.

A peppermint gumleaf floats down from above to settle beside me. I pick it up, put it between my lips. Think of her, the woman I was sure was my soulmate. She smelt like the earth, wholesome. It was a grand thing when we had it. With her I felt more connected than I had ever been, felt that life had real meaning; that together we could take on the world. When we rock climbed and she was belaying, I was empowered and moved surely and swiftly up vertical cliff faces. I had never known such exhilaration in a sport I had pursued for decades.

Touching her after we had reached the top of particularly challenging climbs, the urge to strip her bare of her sweat-soaked clothes overwhelmed me more than once. We made love on clifftops, our bodies sliding together dangerously close to the edge, and both of us more turned on because of it.

I no longer understand the bitterness I felt, the loss. Wasn't it better to have shared that feeling for the time I did than not at all? I feel it now and it sustains me. I have no further need of food. Memories nourish me.

That my body is failing me is of no consequence. This is where I belong. Not in a sanitised place, white walls blocking out the world, electrodes placed on my skull, giving relief for but a short time. Governments and institutions fuck it all up. Put labels on us.

Choice. We should all have choice. I was right to go back to the Franklin some months ago. It was a natural progression to then keep moving south. It's a king's domain, this part of the world, where wilderness rules. I am but a small, transient being in an infinite universe.

The voices in my head have finally quietened, leaving behind my memories. There is no other way for me. This certainty brings a sense of peace; peace I have longed for.

The Boobook calls, 'Oo-hoo, oo-hoo,' heralding the approach of nightfall.

It is nearly time.

thirty-five
# A muddy trail

The slosh, slosh of hiking boots pushing through shallow water is accompanied by our heavy breathing. Sam is ahead of me. I am impressed by his agility and I struggle to keep up. Sweat pools in my eye sockets, and I rub the back of my hand distractedly across my face. Blinking, I pause to take in the impressive dolerite columns flanking Precipitous Bluff. The columns stretch out like a serrated dinosaur tail above the tree line, drawing our eyes to the mountain. It teases us, seemingly near, yet still a day's walk away. The humidity is oppressive. Steely clouds sit at our backs on the southern horizon.

Aware that a blind will soon be pulled down in front of us, that of dusk obscuring visibility, I quicken my pace. Sam walks to a methodical rhythm, his large backpack a reassuring bulk. His renewed strength and sure tread are testimony to the many months of hard work he put in to regain health and fitness. My backpack too is bulky, containing sleeping gear, enough food for several days, and items important on this journey, including the journal I have been making notes in since being reunited with Sam in Hobart.

I started the journal to track Sam's progressive recovery and it quickly became an outlet for my own emotional journey. Writing down my thoughts is good therapy and helps me to make sense of things. As the months went by, I found myself writing about Aaron and his subsequent disappearance. These journal entries contain a lot of question marks. Having not been able to come to terms with the lack of results elicited by search parties, Sam and I had agreed on our own search. If nothing else, we reasoned it would be a good test of Sam's health, and perhaps it would lay some ghosts to rest for me.

'Not far now before we take a break, honey. You'll have to start coming to the gym with me,' Sam says, looking back at me with raised brows. He is full of cheek.

'Maybe I will,' I pant, catching up with him. I chug down some water and pause to take in my surrounds. Tendrils of mist stretch out as haphazardly as seaweed washed up on a shoreline. Soon it will settle into gullies below the bulk of the mountain, tucking into nooks and crannies, ready for the night.

Turning inland to find access across a small creek, I negotiate a rotting tree trunk that is partly disintegrated and sink knee-deep in squelchy mud. Sam is quick to give me a hand, boots sucking at the mud as he hoists me free. We clamber carefully over fallen trees until we are clear of obstacles and stepping through shallow water once more. Water levels are unusually low for autumn and, despite the ever-present mud, we are making good progress. Global warming has some advantages in the short term it would seem, despite our dire environmental forecast.

Today the track became more challenging as we veered inland and walked alongside New River Lagoon. After leaving the Prion Beach campsite in the morning, we were relieved not to get our boots immediately sodden as we negotiated the first few kilometres of the northbound trail. Following the eastern side of the lagoon, we then encountered fallen timber that forced us into shallow water at regular intervals. The entrances of the creek pushed us away from the main water course, leaving us little choice but to go bush in search of negotiable crossing points.

# UNDERTOW

Black pools of water appear bottomless as we skirt across them on a crisscross of fallen tree trunks. All in all, we are lucky; only once or twice have we gone beyond ankle-deep water to make progress. It had been a different story when Aaron had disappeared. Then the lagoon had been swollen from heavy rains.

Our goal for today is to have our tent set up at Cavern Camp before nightfall. Tomorrow we begin our ascent up Precipitous Bluff, all going as planned. Sam and I started our walk from Cockle Creek to New River Lagoon four days ago. We crossed the South Cape rivulet after leaving South East Cape behind us, negotiated the rounded rocks strewn across Granite Beach, and the smooth sand of Surprise Bay, en route to Prion Beach.

While Sam was at the gym, I preferred to train outside in preparation for this trip. Pounding running trails that weave through trees and scrub, I feel more wholly myself, thoughts uninhibited, roaming free. Sometimes I catch up with Maz, who comes to Hobart regularly on days off from her guiding work on the Freycinet Peninsula. We often set off a day's hiking on kunanyi/Mount Wellington. We are never at a loss for words, with much to catch up on. We have the sort of bond that generally takes years to forge in a friendship, and for that I am truly grateful. Our shared experiences give us an empathy that enables us to talk about our personal lives with ease. Maz and Sam clicked as soon as they met. Sam had given her a huge hug, expressing thanks for her efforts in finding help when I was attending to Aaron.

Undertaking this quest on the South Coast, I am reminded again of the unique beauty we have here in Tasmania. In better circumstances and with my own health fully restored (to quote my father, I once more have 'meat on my bones'), I am enjoying the environment all the more. The weather has been calm, though muggy. The scenery en route from Cockle Creek is as stunning as I recall from the first time that Sam and I hiked the South Coast Track, albeit from the other direction. Craggy headlands project into the Southern Ocean and idyllic, protected bays give respite from mud and wet bush. I feel charged with purpose. I hope this trip will help us both to have closure of sorts, and to move on.

A kookaburra cackles, disturbing my musings. A moment's lapse is all it takes for me to put my foot through another rotting branch. My backpack slips and I veer sideways.

'Shit,' I swear, stumbling.

Sam turns abruptly, leaps forward, and reaches out in an effort to steady me. We both fall down in a messy tangle. Sitting in mud is not ideal on a waterlogged trail with darkness descending; still, we are laughing. Helping each other up, we slip and slide like a couple of courting eels. Sam paints a muddy print on my face. His happy disposition is contagious.

Playfully shoving Sam out of the way as our laughter echoes around the bush, I wring out the sodden front of my shirt, hoist my backpack back into position, and push through the scrub to the campground ahead.

thirty-six

# Cavern Camp

It is with relief that we arrive at Cavern Camp. The dry campsite is welcoming in the cool of late afternoon and we quickly find a level piece of ground on which to set up our tent. A pademelon is reluctant to move, as it sits with an air of proprietary on the prime piece of real estate. It hops away at a leisurely pace as I kick mammal poo aside in readiness to empty our backpacks. It's not just shrugging off my pack that has made me feel lighter, although I do so with relief. The simple task of putting one booted foot in front of another when hiking has always helped to restore my sense of equilibrium.

I take off my boots with relief, as they are wet through after wading through water for much of the day. Our clothes are not in much better shape. I stretch my arms above my head, flex my back, and look around the campsite.

'Give us a hand, Kay,' calls Sam, throwing me a bag of tent pegs and snapping me out of my reverie.

A restless energy prickles and niggles me. Damper Cave is only a short walk from the campground and I impulsively decide to check out the entrance before the day is done. At first light tomorrow Sam and I plan to enter the cave and explore it as thoroughly as conditions allow us to. Although permanently damp, lack of recent rain will hopefully allow for an extensive search of the cave's chambers.

It was in the cave that Gary and his fellow search and rescue crew found the one piece of physical evidence suggestive of Aaron's presence in the area: a tobacco pouch. The uncommon brand was the same Aaron smoked, yet while I was convinced Aaron had been in the cave, Gary was cautious in jumping to any conclusions. I conceded that someone else who smoked the same brand of tobacco as Aaron could have been in the cave, however, the timing of the find and a gut feeling left me with little doubt that the empty pouch was my friend's. Sam, long used to my instincts being pretty spot on, had not argued with my theory. Convincing Gary had been another matter.

When the search for Aaron had been called off, Gary had come to visit Sam and me. He was both direct and empathetic – a balance fine-tuned after years of rescue work – as he told me that searchers had failed to find any further conclusive trace of Aaron after the initial footprints, and therefore the search had been discontinued. An object found in Damper Cave was the only tangible sign of anyone having been in the area in recent months. It was then that he told me about the tobacco pouch, although he must have instantly regretted it given my heightened excitement. I could not fault the dedication of Gary and fellow search and rescue personnel. My appreciation of the time and effort put in by search parties was not lessened by the lack of results.

I was disappointed and fell into a despondent mood at times, particularly when I spent too much time pondering Aaron's whereabouts. Days shortened with the onset of winter, and it was a good thing that I had plenty to occupy my mind. I focused on Sam's recovery, my own recovery from the ordeal I had gone through, and on spending time with family. There have been many joyous family get-togethers since my return.

My mental scars are just as real as Sam's physical ones. Time with family has helped me to heal. It took many months to sleep soundly again. I still have nightmares of eerie fog closing in on me and squeezing the breath out of my lungs. I rejoice in simple things like never before; waking up in my own bed, flicking the switch on the kettle, knowing I am safe.

'If Aaron did want to be found he would have left something to point us in the right direction,' Sam mumbles, pushing aside bushes as he fossicks around.

I hope Sam is right. 'I'm going to go for a quick walk to check out the entrance to the cave.'

He looks at me in surprise. 'Can't that wait till morning?'

'A quick look-see only and I'll be back,' I tell him.

Sam shrugs in resignation. 'Just don't be long, and tuck your EPIRB into your coat pocket, okay?' We're both wary of separation in wilderness after our respective ordeals.

'By the time you make a cuppa, I'll be back.' I give him a quick kiss and start off down the track.

Access to the cave is through a creek emerging from the entrance. Our boots will have little time to dry overnight before our foray into the cave. A fluttering of excitement catches me off guard. I might finally be close to finding some answers. My instincts are telling me so, more loudly the closer to Damper Cave I get. Perhaps something was missed and we will find another clue, something to help indicate Aaron's intentions. If not, at least I will finally be able to say I did all I could to uncover the truth of his disappearance.

Aaron's family members, who I have spoken to on a number of occasions over mugs of rich coffee – a family preference, for sure – deserve answers. They accepted the story of my time with Aaron in wilderness readily enough, being acutely aware of Aaron's maverick nature and his tendency to isolate himself, however were both surprised and saddened to learn of his illness. To not have the opportunity to say goodbye to those we love makes loss all the more heart-wrenching.

After I was rescued and flown to Hobart with Matt, the weather had deteriorated and the search for Aaron had been called off forty-eight hours after it had begun. A week later a search party had set out from Cockle Creek, walking this same route to Precipitous Bluff. A search of the main cave had been made, as far as the high-water levels then had allowed. Smaller tunnels branch out from inside Damper, narrow, low-roofed and hard to negotiate – near impossible after heavy rains.

'Fit for wombats only,' Gary had declared.

Continuing on to Precipitous Bluff and finishing the circuit at Lune River, no further trace of Aaron's presence had been found. It was then that Gary had come to see me and announce they could do no more.

At the cave entrance I sit on a log tinged green with moss. The afternoon shadows have lengthened, stretching out into dark shapes before me. Aaron's image readily comes to mind and I can almost see him sitting here in his customary pose, legs bent at sharp angles, long hair falling over his face. Closing my eyes, I see Aaron open the tobacco pouch in his hand, movements slow and deliberate.

*Did you light a cigarette here and accidently drop the tobacco pouch?*
*Were you distracted as you stood to go into the cave?*
*What was your plan?*
*What happened?*

Hairs prickle my neck. I stand abruptly, brush myself off, and walk briskly back along the path. Morning will come soon enough, and when it does Sam and I will come back here together and venture into the cave.

Wet ferns slap at my arms and face as I scurry away from the cave. I flick my headtorch on as the waning light makes navigation increasingly difficult on the narrow track. I pause to let a possum, momentarily stunned, adjust to my presence before scampering off into the bushes. The forest closes in on me protectively as the last of the daylight retreats into dense bush.

Back at camp I fall into Sam's arms, surprising him. I am relieved to have him on my team, secure in his belief and am grateful not to be doing this alone.

'I felt something at the cave. I could honestly feel Aaron's presence,' I say, shivering a little.

With his arms wrapped around me, I snuggle into Sam's chest, then pull back as I inadvertently wipe my wet and dirty face on his shirt.

'Oh, it's like that is it?' he declares in mock outrage.

I voice an unconvincing protest as he paints the front of my shirt with muddy hand prints in turn. Once more in the southern wilderness with Sam, in the place where I had first realised I was in love with my best friend, desire – long dormant after trauma – is resurfacing. I pull Sam's shirt free of his pants and run my hands under the rough cloth. His eyebrows arch in surprise, but when I smile, he is fast to whip my shirt aside. We barely have our boots off before we are falling backwards into the tent.

Afterwards, my head on Sam's bare chest, I trace my fingers down his torso and around the lines of his hips, feeling the familiar contours of his body. The night breeze whispers outside as we lay entwined in our joined sleeping bags. Sam is as steadfast as the mountain above us and for this, and all I have, I give silent thanks. The sounds of bush critters foraging under cover of darkness blend with Sam's gentle snoring. It is comforting, and despite the myriad of thoughts dancing in my head and flutters of excitement as to what a new day will bring, I can feel myself starting to drift into sleep.

thirty-seven

# Damper Cave

A linear stretch of gold splits the soft pink sky. In the cool of first light, I fire up the jet boil and sit back to await my morning cuppa. Emanating from our tent is a low-pitched whistling, which is the sound Sam makes when he is in deep sleep. A fairy wren hops around the tent, tilting its little head in a comical fashion as it listens intently to the foreign sound penetrating through nylon walls. Incongruous as it is in this remote location, the tent is accepted by bush creatures as a new addition to the environment. Sam's snores are a curiosity.

Shaking my head with a smile, I splash water into my battered tin mug, a relic from bygone hiking trips. The tea steeps, resembling the colour of the lagoon which I glimpse through the trees. This is my favourite way to start the day; with a brew, in the bush, birdsong providing morning music. Sunlight slides thin fingers between the trees as I cup my warm mug of tea in my hands and take a sip. I raise my head and breathe in the clear mountain air; the freshness of morning. While this routine is calming, today there is a persistent fluttering inside me as I anticipate entering Damper Cave.

A kookaburra sits in the branch above me, its oversized head pivoting comically on a short neck, dark eyes focusing on the ground. A lizard darts under the log I am sitting on. That option is no longer on the kookaburra's breakfast menu – loud cackling erupts as the disgruntled bird flies off to search elsewhere for breakfast. I'm scrounging through our supplies for a bag of oats when I see Sam's head appear through the tent flap.

'Geez, Kay, you must be freezing your butt off!' he exclaims, engulfing me in a generous hug and rubbing my back vigorously.

God how I had missed Sam's ability to make me laugh during his long months of recovery. Clad as I am in my underwear, long-sleeved thermal top and knickers, I admit to being a tad chilled in my hindquarters. Bush fashion. I have hung my damp and dirty hiking pants on a tree branch, optimistically hoping that sun and breeze will at least go partway to drying them. Sam wraps his coat around my legs and gives me a quick rubdown – 'Necessary for warmth,' he states with confidence, and a wink – before we sit together to eat our breakfast. I am indeed warmed.

We dip our spoons into bowls of steaming porridge. An echidna appears at the edge of the campground and sniffs the air with its nosey snout, then retreats back in to the bushes. Currawongs sing their morning song and all around us insects flutter, captured in sunbeams as daylight filters through the trees.

We hoist on our backpacks and set out from Cavern Camp. Sam takes my hand and threads his fingers through mine. Walking along the trail together, we absorb the environment surrounding us, saying little; both of us lost in our own thoughts. Morning dew weighs on tree ferns and we're showered with droplets of moisture as we brush past them. Approaching the cave entrance, I feel a drop in temperature and shiver as I contemplate wading inside. A stream feeds lush vegetation at the mouth of the cave, the dinosaur-shaped hump of Precipitous Bluff a black silhouette above us; a benevolent giant on watch. Birds go about their business and a gentle rain begins to fall. A millipede crosses our path, multiple legs creating a time lapsed wave of energy that pushes it forward.

Aaron has been here – I know it. Closing my eyes, I breathe in the wet, heady smell of the bush, dank water, and something else; intangible, but present in a very real sense to me. I close my eyes and the aroma of Aaron's marijuana-laced cigarettes comes back to me. A sense of coming full circle, of completing a journey, pervades. The flush of anticipation I feel intensifies.

We rest our backpacks by the log at the entrance and pull on our wet weather gear. The cave will be damp and cool. Sam retrieves a few items from his pack, including rope and glowsticks, and puts them into a small backpack he brought along for just this purpose. Ensuring my gaiters are securely attached to my hiking boots, beanie pulled low and headtorch on, I follow Sam under the fern fringed entrance. It reassures me that Sam thought to pack a caving rope and that we are now attached to one another. The rope will feed out as we walk, and I don't intend to let us move too far apart. Claustrophobia that usually holds me back from entering enclosed spaces is not a factor this morning, as I have far too much adrenaline coursing through me to linger.

Sloshing through the opening of the cave, we pause to take in the convoluted stalactites that form a sculptural gallery above us. It is an impressive sight, and Sam and I gaze in rapt wonder. A cricket appears from a crack in the wall, quickly retreating. Lush green vegetation is reflected in the water, picture perfect. The stalactites are waxen and appear to be freeze-framed. Now that we are in the cave I don't want to rush and miss anything. Hence, despite the cold walls closing in on me, I plod along slowly, my head swivelling back and forth like one of those open-mouthed clown heads at an amusement park.

'Come on, Kay. Let's go,' Sam calls over his shoulder.

The main chamber of the cave is larger than I had anticipated. As we slosh through water, we shine our headtorches in wide arcs around the walls. Small burrow-like openings are dotted all around the chamber and some we are able to scramble up to and peer inside. I can understand the reference to wombats now, although many of the holes look barely big enough for a rat to squeeze through.

We disturb a bat which gets as much of a fright as we do, its sharp wings tipping as it does a hard turn and is lost in darkness. Around fifty metres inside the cave, which we are carefully negotiating while walking single file through the creek, we shine our torches upwards and spy a small elevated passage around my shoulder height. Sam hoists me up and we are soon in the passage following a pebbly trench, just wide enough for our bodies to squeeze through. I crouch to make progress and am careful not to hit my head on the rock ceiling above us. Several minutes later we are still moving forward in the passage, which has not narrowed any further, nor has it widened. I am starting to feel claustrophobic. My breathing is quicker and sweat is trickling down my back.

'Let's head back,' I call, jerking the line that attaches us. Sam hears the waver in my voice and is quick to agree.

Rotating my body around, the torch shines on a curved section of wall, beyond which is a partly-concealed entrance to a cavernous space, several feet below the overhang where I am standing. It's easy to miss. A slippery-looking descent would have to be negotiated to investigate further. Crickets scurry back as the beam sweeps around the cavern below, which is as large as my lounge room back home. About to move on, something catches my attention. If I had not paused, I would have missed what my torch beam is fixed on.

Crouching down, I carefully lean over and focus the beam on oddly-shaped objects strewn below. I can't decipher what I am looking at. A ledge projects under where I am crouched. I shine my torch along its length. My heart jumps in my chest as light dances off bleached bones.

I jerk back and scream as my headtorch falls, bouncing into the darkness below. A wild arc of light picks up rock, dust, and the bones.

'Sam, I've found something!' My voice booms around the cavern below me.

Sam is quickly at my side, trying to reassure me, but I feel his tension. 'It's okay, it's just animal bones. I'll check it out.'

I nod my head dumbly. The beam from his torch dances off dark rock walls as he prepares to slide down into the cavern. No way am I staying where I am in the dark.

'Wait! I'm coming, too.'

The descent into the cavern is slippery and I lean backwards, keeping my feet wide for balance and in an effort not to fall forward. With an ungainly thud I am on the floor of the cavern beside Sam. Projecting his light towards the ledge, I hear Sam give a sharp intake of breath and direct my gaze to where he is looking.

Under the overhang above, the ledge extends into a deep rock shelf. The shelf is strewn with bones. Beyond and clearly defined in the beam lies a bundle of cloth. A lone hiking boot sits at an awkward angle at the end of the bundle. It looks a lot like the type of boot that Aaron wears. This time my scream reverberates off the walls of the cavern, assaulting my eardrums.

Sam pulls me into his arms, trying to calm me. He is trembling, too. 'Just stay put Kay, please.'

He tentatively approaches the shelf, inching his hand up towards the cloth. Hesitating, he turns to me. I nod, terrified of what he may reveal but knowing we have come too far to shirk away. He lifts the corner of what is unmistakably an old sleeping bag. I gasp. The sleeping bag too is familiar. A coat sleeve lies in lazy repose. From my position beside Sam, I struggle to fully comprehend what I am looking at.

*Is it possible? Could it really be?*

Sam pulls the sleeping bag further aside. Dust rises like a dirty cloud and disperses, and we turn our backs to cough. As the dust settles, what lies beneath can no longer be denied. Sam lets his hand drop and stumbles backwards, toppling me so that we both fall sideways. He lands on top of me and, as I scramble from under him, my hand finds his headtorch on the ground beside us. I secure it on my head and shine the beam towards the shelf.

The light dances before it settles in a hard stare on the decomposed body before us. The Devils may have feasted, scattering bones in their wake, but a human form is nonetheless distinguishable.

It is Aaron's remains.

thirty-eight
# A resting place

I kneel in stunned silence. Sadness weighs heavily as I try to absorb the loss of my friend. Sam looks as shocked as I am as he takes my face between his cupped hands, looks into my eyes with unspoken sympathy, and places his forehead against mine.

For long minutes we sit this way, until Sam stands and reaches into his backpack. Taking out two glowsticks, he snaps both and gives them a shake to reveal a slow, burning light. Placing them on the ground in front of the shelf, the scene before us seems even more surreal as Aaron's remains take on a luminous glow.

'This is the spot he chose. For whatever reason. I think we should honour that.'

Sam nods in a gesture of understanding and agreement. We stand with arms wrapped around each other for several long minutes.

I know we have reached a mutual decision when Sam and I lock eyes. We have no need of words. For the present, Aaron's remains will stay in the resting place he chose, Damper Cave. We cannot control whatever decisions are made by family and authorities at a later date. Here, now, Sam and I will respect his decisions as best we can. If he wanted to be found, he would not be here.

Sam is careful as he retrieves the disturbed bones. He places them with the other skeletal remains inside the old sleeping bag. I pick up Aaron's solitary hiking boot and place it on top of the mounded sleeping bag. My hands are shaking so much I nearly drop the boot. Well-worn and travel weary, I can think of no more fitting alternative to a headstone than this. What happened to the other boot, I will never know. Had he lost it pushing through water en route to here? I choke down a sob of raw emotion. I don't like to think of anyone dying alone.

'Maybe his family will come here one day, put a memorial outside the cave,' I say quietly.

Sam wraps his arms around me from behind, resting his head on top of mine. We are silent as we look towards the shelf. Aaron's ravaged body now lies neatly tucked inside his sleeping bag, a hiking boot sitting on top, like a mountaineer standing proudly atop a summit. Job done.

By the time I met Aaron, I believe he had come to terms with his mental and physical afflictions and was at a place of acceptance, finding great solace in nature. When sharing his knowledge of the bush with me, he was at his brightest, animated and even joyful. He knew the botanical name of every plant we encountered. He could identify birds and insects readily and was a walking historian, his love of the South Western Wilderness obvious.

'I want to say something to farewell Aaron, but I don't know if I can find the words,' I snuffle, face pressed against Sam's shirt.

'Let's not say anything then. Just remember, Kay. That's a tribute in itself.'

I bow my head and Sam does likewise in silent tribute to Aaron – my friend – a unique and caring man.

Squeezing my eyes tightly shut I recall how Aaron looked as he had stood in the shallows at Prion Beach. Sunlight had caught water droplets as he shook his long hair side to side and arched his reed thin body towards the sky. Remembering his calm smile and demeanour, I acknowledge that Aaron had accepted his death and planned for its imminence. He had swum in the ocean and eaten what may have been his last meal. The swim and the food had replenished his body and spirit for the journey ahead. I believe Aaron was most likely on a quest to reach Precipitous Bluff when his body failed him. Aaron had great mental strength, of that there was no doubt. That he had made it as far as he had when so ill is testimony to the man he was.

The glow lights are beginning to dim as I place my hand on Aaron's makeshift headstone in quiet farewell. I find a lighter discarded under the shelf as I am having a final look around the chamber. It is Aaron's. I look towards his burial place as I place it in my pocket and take a deep breath. 'Rest in peace, my friend.'

Rather than sound trite, the words are entirely perfect. True friendship is not measured in lengths of time, it is measured in worth. Aaron had played an important role in my life and I valued him greatly. I cannot change the outcome but I can honour Aaron's memory and finally give his family closure after what we have discovered here today.

Wearily we tread the path back to Cavern Camp. There is no point going any further up the mountain. The forest is unusually quiet, respectful of death. Sam and I readily agree that a man who had chosen to enter a partially-flooded cave – as I imagined it must have been then – to find a concealed chamber and position himself thus on a hidden ledge, was a man who chose his burial place with deliberation. I may not understand Aaron's decisions, but I can respect his choices, and his bravery. I brush aside wet vegetation, moisture spraying in sunbeams in front of me. I feel for the lighter in my pocket at regular intervals.

## UNDERTOW

Arriving back at camp, I make straight for the lagoon. The birds sing a sweet welcome and eucalyptus trees sway in the afternoon breeze. The world goes about its business. I choose a rock to sit on and look out over the water. The soft light is a balm for my unsettled mind. I sit for a long time, watching as the sun lowers in the western sky. The sunset is muted by a veil of clouds, brilliance hinted at by a red outline above Precipitous Bluff, as daylight succumbs to the inevitable. Darkness slides in for the night and dazzling rays pierce the bruised clouds above. High in the sky clouds pull apart to reveal a portal of white light. I do not need to touch Aaron's lighter now to feel him close to me.

Aaron chose to die away from the blaring, grating noises and confusion that human habitation invariably brings, instead seeking the peace that nature offers. His body has given sustenance to animals, as is the natural order of things. Life and death, an intrinsic cycle.

A soft breeze fans my cheeks, insects buzz around me, and as I gaze upwards the first star of the night appears. Aaron's remains are tucked inside his sleeping bag in Damper Cave; his spirit free to roam in the mountains, forests, and ravines of the Southern Tasmanian wilderness. He is home in nature's embrace.

thirty-nine
# The Ironbound Range

Mountain peaks rise and fall, stretching into the distance as far as the eye can see. The view is majestic from our vantage point. We are perched on a rocky outcrop on the summit of the Ironbound Range. The range is like a big speedhump between Turua Beach and Louisa River, rising straight up from the sea to a height of just under 1000 metres. Two wedge-tailed eagles perform aerobatics in the distance, one above the other, soaring over folds of mountains that pucker like blankets pushed aside.

Mugs of tea in hand, Sam and I settle to enjoy the sun on our shoulders, dipping Scotch Finger biscuits into our cuppas. We agree we are fortunate to have had clear weather both times we have crossed this mountain range. Federation Peak, with its distinctive jagged summit, rises above the other peaks, the jewel on a crown of multi-layered mountains. Each layer is another shade of blue, softening on the horizon where land and sky meet. Pierced by shards of light, remnants of shredded clouds stretch like gossamer scarves, weaving through valleys. Sam's ropey forearm is draped over my shoulder as he plants a kiss on my nose. We have been through a lot and time is needed to process events, and to heal. I am so grateful that we have each other. Turning my face to his, our lips meet.

Not even the raucous cry of currawongs squabbling over biscuit crumbs can disturb the moment. Sam does not rush

## UNDERTOW

as he unbuttons my shirt, never taking his eyes from mine. A fresh wave of desire washes over me. Our bodies fit together perfectly, as nature intends for all unions that are meant to be. With my head buried against Sam's firm shoulder, I feel his muscles twitch, alive and tasting of salt and the sea. I tease that he must have been a sea creature in a previous life, so at home is he in the water. Arching my body upwards I see the blue sky winking at me as Sam buries his face in my neck.

---

I'm lying beside Sam on the sparse patch of grass when a breeze washes over us. Sam gathers me in his arms and kisses me with great tenderness. We snuggle together until goosebumps tickle our skin, then quickly dress. It is time to ensure we are set up for the night in case the wind picks up.

High camp is exposed to the elements, at just under 900 metres in altitude, and we are relieved to have calm weather, enabling us to set up our tent here. There is no way I could have made it to the next campsite at Louisa River tonight and am hoping the weather favours us a little longer. There is a front moving over the state from the west later in the week and we are keen to beat it. After the two days we took to hike here from the cave, and our ascent up the steep steps of the mountain today, rolling out our sleeping bags holds great appeal.

'Just in case we do get wind tonight, I'll put a couple of extra lines on the tent,' Sam says as I am rummaging in my pack for the stove.

We commenced retracing our steps south from Cavern Camp at first light the day after finding Aaron's remains. Having put in a long day's walk, by the time we set up camp at Turua Beach to the west of New River Lagoon, I was both physically and emotionally exhausted. My feet were rubbed raw after trudging through water in my hiking boots yet again. I can't even remember going to bed. When I woke up, I saw familiar landmarks as we were close to where Aaron and I had camped many months ago.

Memories had hit me like a sledge hammer. My head and heart were overwhelmed and I had cried while lamenting the fact that we were still some days from home. I just wanted to be in my own bed with the doona pulled up over me. Sam did his best to comfort me and had the camp packed up in record time so that we could move on.

From the Ironbound Range it is a walk of only a few more days before we reach Melaleuca and can catch a flight back to Hobart. Before leaving Cavern Camp we had used our satellite phone to call Gary and advise him of the discovery of Aaron's body. Gary had been gobsmacked and said he would call Aaron's family immediately. However, the only people who can recount all the details to them are Sam and I. It will be a hard conversation.

Since Turua Beach I have found my hiking rhythm and have slowed down my pace. There is comfort to be had in putting one foot in front of another, and as I move forward my tread is becoming lighter. Finding Aaron's remains was both shocking and, in a bizarre way, a relief. I believe his family will feel likewise. Not knowing weighs heavily.

Low clouds on the western horizon hint at cooler days ahead as the sun sinks towards the mountains. It is a form of meditation, letting thoughts drift and flow, much as the ocean does at our backs below the Ironbound Ranges. Forrest Gump famously said, 'Life is like a box of chocolates.' For me it is more akin to mountain peaks and the hidden valleys below. Sometimes the view is clear; at other times it is dark and mysterious.

Sam is already snoring by the time I crawl into my sleeping bag. He has collapsed without bothering to get undressed. Cold air licks at my body as I strip off my clothes. Nestling against Sam's back, I feel like I am the only person awake in the vastness of the South Western Wilderness. An intense longing to be sitting at Mum and Dad's kitchen table catches me by surprise. Dad has a knack for bringing me down to earth, and I bask in Mum's care and attention. Whenever I need normalisation, I find myself on the road to my parents' house. Driving through the gates to their property, I wind around the driveway to the back of the house to see them waiting for me on the doorstep. I hope I will be greeted in the same way for many years to come.

Morning. Standing to face the blue rolling mountain ranges, Sam's hand is firm in mine. Frenchmans Cap to the west is just visible in the distance. It is a special place in the world where one can see a mountain hundreds of kilometres away from a vantage point. No road, building, or sign of human interference is visible to us as we start our descent down the Ironbound Range. As I look over the mountains, I imagine Aaron's spirit flying free over a landscape that time has forgotten.

Louisa River, our camp for the night, lies way down below. At least the downhill will be a nice contrast to yesterday's uphill walking, although I suspect our knees and feet will suffer.

Sam starts singing an old song, a sea ballad he sings at times to me to make me smile. He has not sung since his accident and a shiver of quiet joy runs through me. I pause to look at this wonderful man who has defied the odds and survived a harrowing sea ordeal to come home to me. His voice is rich, the song melodic, and as he gains pitch, his voice takes flight.

forty
# A new day

A Jack Jumper races perilously close to my toes. I draw my knees up to my chest, hugging them and resting my chin on jean-clad knees. Gannets dive with knife-like precision and a sea eagle sweeps the sky to an invisible conductor's commands. The river continues to withdraw from the shoreline, soldier crabs scurry, and a heron daintily hops between the red masses.

Our neighbour has dragged his kayak up on the beach before the tide retreated, its path a fingernail line on the wet sand. Gum leaves rustle in the new day breeze and the sun is gaining bulk as it noses above the ranges. Spreading gold across the waterways, I watch as sunlight reaches the low-lying peninsula of Dolphin Sands across the river from us. The morning holds the promise of a warm day.

The more peaceful way of life here on the Freycinet Peninsula – known as poyananu by the Aboriginal people who inhabited the land long before Europeans – has justified our decision to move away from the city. Hobart is only a few hours south by car, and yet on mornings like this the city's hustle and bustle seems much further away.

A pelican skids in to rest on the shallow sandbank stretching out from the far shore. Fish splash in a feeding frenzy close to the surface and the pelican takes flight as it sees the chance of a feed. It appears to be running on water momentarily, beating its wings madly before rising into the air. It never fails to astound me how such a bulky bird flies with such ease.

Tig, our six-month-old puppy, is frantically digging at the base of bushes close by. She is a funny little thing, her antics a constant source of delight. We had gone to the lost dog's home to pick out a pup, but really Tig chose us. How could we resist the little Jack Russel when those big brown eyes pleaded with us, 'Pick me!'?

Tig has a neat trick of standing on her front legs to urinate. Now there's a party trick! Sandpiper Beach is her favourite place in the world, where she gets to run free, unleashed and without our constant cries of, 'Come back, Tig!' Sam is training her at home, but she is inclined to ignore him on occasion and go bush to play hide-and-seek with the rabbits, and to explore. Her love of the outdoors matches ours and she is the perfect addition to our family.

The hike on the South Coast had revealed much. Our arrival at Melaleuca seemed to punctuate a story ending. We closed the book. Or so we thought.

In reality, it will always be with us, on a shelf right alongside all of our other books. Except this is a book only Sam and I can see, and to which both of us have contributed to. It is the story of the last year of our lives, with chapters missing, a drowning – of *Mulwala* – and a death. As only Aaron could have filled in some of the missing details, I have accepted that what we found at Damper Cave has given me answers enough. His family expressed gratitude and quiet dignity when Sam and I broke the news of our discovery. They declined my offer to guide them to where we found Aaron's body.

These days we speak little about our personal ordeals, nor discuss our time at Damper Cave, needing time to come to terms with all that has happened over the course of this past year. Sometimes I pause to look at a photo Sam took of me on our hike. It sits on our bookshelf. In the photo, I am leaning out over the rocky outcrop where I scattered flowers in memory of Aaron. The Ironbound Range seemed the perfect place to pay my respects. It stands alone, yet is surrounded by the best nature has to offer. It is a good photo. I am smiling, the mountains clear as they fold and fade behind me.

After arriving back home, Sam and I have gone about our day-to-day work and lives quietly. Travelling the road back and forth to Hobart, I am constantly reminded of what a privilege it is to live in such a picturesque part of the world. We take long walks on the beach with Tig, and I spend time on the river in my kayak, enjoying calm water and the birdlife. After dinner we watch sitcoms, losing ourselves in a world of make-believe where good endings are the norm.

Sam evidently made a decision about our own 'happy ending'. Or, perhaps he was thinking more along the lines of a new year and happy beginnings? He proposed a big New Year's Eve party, formal up top, bogan down below. Sam has always enjoyed theme parties and once won the party award when he dressed up as Gilligan and took on a persona hard to fault. He does make me laugh.

I look down at my feet, making circles in the sandy soil. I will paint my toenails for today's occasion. Sam leans over the back of the seat, his arms encircling me, smile wide. 'Good morning, lovely one,' he whispers in my ear.

I turn to kiss him. Excitement bubbles up within me and I splutter into my mug of tea. Sam has outdone himself with his attire and is wearing a tuxedo with the pants rolled up, minus footwear, and has donned a top hat.

'Well, good morning to you too, sir.'

A blue dress adorned with tiny white sailboats patterned around its calf-length hem is hung ready to wear in the bedroom. The dress is perfect. I could not believe my luck when I saw it hanging in the shop window of the seaside town of Bicheno. Sasha had been with me; as if my daughter would miss out on a shopping trip. It was a fun outing.

Sam and I cannot repress our delight. To see family and so many of our friends together at our new home will be such fun, and most definitely a celebration of what is most important to us. A ripple flutters over the water as we watch. Content to start the day slowly, our hands meet in the middle of the seat as we drink our tea and chat about the day ahead.

The breeze pushes the ripple into the deeper part of the river channel where it momentarily becomes a darker blanket, hastily tossed. The white and yellow catamaran bobs merrily as it tugs at the mooring line. When we had first moved into this beach house the boat had been owned by a neighbour. It had intrigued me, so pretty did she look on the river. We had been invited to sail on the small catamaran, and while Sam had declined, I had been keen to give it a go. The sea, slow to entice when Sam had first introduced me to sailing, beckons me still.

On that first trip out on the catamaran, the then-boat owners and I had sailed into Great Oyster Bay and continued on to the furthermost tip of the Freycinet Peninsula before cutting across the passage to Schouten Island. We had sailed past Hazards Beach, a pristine white strip, beyond which lies The Hazards Mountain range consisting of five rugged peaks joined at the hip, with a wow factor that attracts summer tourists. Sometimes the mountains take on a reddish glow, as if embarrassed by their own splendour.

I can see them in the distance through our kitchen window. They give me a clue, as if peering through a looking glass, as to what the weather will be like for the day. When the weather comes from the east, cloud hugs the rocky peaks and I cross my fingers that my vegetable patch will get a good drenching.

Freycinet is a dry region and houses on the isolated peninsula rely on tank water. Rain is celebrated, as it has always been.

We had gone through the passage in the little catamaran, leaving behind the protected bay and sailing out into the ocean. As we left the peninsula and Schouten Island behind, my heartrate had increased. It was a momentary response and I quickly calmed, revelling in the sense of freedom that had won me over and made a sailor out of me. Seals leapt out of the water in a show of activity. Crested terns tried to emulate gannets, but made more splash as they dove for their breakfast, and seagulls wheeled.

The rain did nothing to dampen our spirits. I simply pulled up the hood of my jacket and tilted my head back to drink from the sky. Later that day we dropped anchor at Schouten Island. Once the rain shower had passed, we had lunch on deck, the rugged contours of the island providing a stunning backdrop. We had the anchorage to ourselves, along with birds flying overhead and stingrays that darted under the boat in impossibly clear water. A sense of peace had enveloped me. I had missed sailing and where it could take me. I made an offer on the boat.

I have named my boat *Albatross*. With a fresh coat of paint and yellow trimmings, *Albatross* is a pretty thing. While Sam makes our morning cuppas, I sit up in bed and watch the river come to life. I never tire of seeing my little boat awaiting me. Matt has been for a sail with me and, as his own boat has a tiller, he has taught me the finer art of tiller steerage. I can handle the catamaran quite easily on my own but prefer sailing in sheltered waters for the time being. I love the feel of wind in my hair, trimming the sails, working the tiller. It feels natural to be out on the water again, in my own boat, no one to interrupt my thoughts – just me and my surrounds.

The ten-metre charter boat Sam and I operate has big outboard motors, and no sails. We are able to get our guests out on the peninsula quickly so that they have a good amount of time to enjoy the area. We specialise in wildlife tours and have got to know where the seals haul out and the best beaches to drop anchor for swimming, picnicking, and playing ashore. Our days off usually include pulling on our hiking boots for a walk somewhere on the peninsula. We have found a balance that works for us. Life is good.

The slap of lines as they whip about in a gust of wind draws our eyes towards *Albatross*. We watch the ruffling of the river as it spreads from the boat to the shallows below our seat, set above the water's edge. It is time to get on with our day.

Matt agrees as he breaks our reverie and plonks down between us. He has made it back from a research voyage to Antarctica in time for the party, and he is ready for it. His excitement at having set foot on the ice at the bottom of the world is contagious. Adventure is in the blood, it seems. As Sasha is wont to say, 'Apples don't fall far from the tree.'

Matt is more of a thrill seeker than me but if I voice such, he is quick to rebuke the claim, stating that leaping off the bow of a sinking yacht to swim to an island is as wild as it gets. He reminds me of our family's good survival instincts. Not that I need reminding. Yes, we are a tough lot, no doubt about that.

My daughter's fingers brush against my neck as she combs my hair. It is all that I could have hoped for to have both of my children here for this day, and the week ahead. 'Time to get dressed, Mum,' commands Sasha, dragging me off the seat with both hands.

She wants to put my make up on for me, and I gladly oblige her. She is far more stylish than I, and I know I will look my best under her ministrations. We put our dresses on together. Sasha looks gorgeous in her dark shimmering dress, and as she spins around, I catch the light reflected in her eyes. She is in love, and I can't wait to meet the lucky man. Already she is talking about children and the future. Time will tell. As long as she is happy, I am too.

The soft material of my dress brushes my thighs as I step onto the deck, then descend the steps to the sand. Dad and Mum are close behind me. I watch as he helps her down the steps and supports her as she leans over to pull off her shoes. I have never seen so many people on our little stretch of beach; family, neighbours, and friends new and old. Most have their shoes off. Maz is out there on the sand, enchanted by the oyster catchers and the river on a beautiful day.

A honeyeater sings a lively tune, lively conversation disturbs the quiet of the day and laughter rings out over the water. Matt has organised some music on the beach and now puts on a very appropriate eighties track. Sam's eyes never leave mine as he takes my hands, and we start to slow dance right there on the sand. Sasha lets out a sigh and Mum starts to cry happy tears. Dad walks over and puts out his hand to Mum.

The party is picking up volume. I dance with Sam, my mother, father, Matt, Sasha, and Maz. My feet are sore. I steal some quiet minutes alone and walk down the path to the beach. Strolling along the tide line, I am surprised when I look up and see how far I have walked. I look out over the water and listen to its whispered blessings. In a moment of impulse, I unzip my dress and let it drop to the sand. The sand is cool underfoot and I like the texture of it against my soles. This part of the beach is deserted. Most of the homeowners on our street are at our party, and tourists generally stick to the main township and nearby national park. I walk out into the water, feeling its caress as it reaches my thighs. The tide has started to come in; even so, I wade quite a distance before I can dive into the deeper channel.

Down I dive, scooping water aside as I descend into the cooling depths. Holding my breath, I swim close to the river floor, brushing the soft seagrass with my fingers. Even though my lungs are nearly bursting, I roll over and let the current take me. I look towards the surface of the water where ribbons of light rush away from me. Silver fish flash past my face.

I close my eyes and feel everything.

# Acknowledgments

This book would not have been possible without the input of many. Thank you to all those mentioned below, and to the many who are not.

When researching material for this book, I spoke with Damian Bidgood, who worked for the Tasmania Police Search and Rescue team for 24 years, and who generously donated his time for a lengthy interview. His first-hand knowledge of Pedra Branca was instrumental in setting the scene for the first chapters of this book. I gratefully acknowledge, thank, and pay respect to all Tasmania Police Search and Rescue personnel, including Scotty Dunn and Steve Williams.

The hardy fishermen who work the waters in the Southern Ocean and who braved the re-telling of their adventures at sea, deserve acknowledgment likewise. A special mention goes to Sam Greggs and James Parkinson.

Writers are not easy to live with, even less so when sharing a small space. Kerry lived with me aboard our vessel, *Yarrakai*, for seven years. Together we sailed and hiked in Tasmanian wilderness regions, and out of our adventures this novel was born. I give thanks to Kerry for his unfailing patience and support during my writing journey, and intimate knowledge of the sea, boats and Tasmanian waterways. Those years were a gift.

To the readers of earlier drafts of *Undertow*, I thank you all for your time, feedback and, unfailingly, your belief in my story.

Thank you to my friend, Karen Wilson-Megahan, for my author photograph. A big thank you goes to Doug Thost for my book cover photograph. Both are talented and generous people.

Although *Undertow* is a work of fiction, some places and characters may bear resemblance to actual places and people. I give thanks to the persons who allowed me to develop characters from my interactions with them. A special mention goes to, Rob Hayes, a fellow sailor and bushman. I greatly respect his passion for, and care and understanding of, Tasmanian wilderness regions.

A big thank-you goes to my friend, structural editor and mentor, Les Zig. Les gave me guidance and bolstered me many times over the years it took to write Undertow. He is an exceptional editor who gives generously of his time to support fellow writers. Without Les, my story would still be a work in progress.

I give thanks to my copy-editor, Laura McCluskey, who helped me to pull it all together and polish my novel in readiness for publication. Her flexibility, expertise and generosity ensured the end result was all I could have wished it to be. Thank you also to Melita Eagling, who helped in the early stages of copy-editing my book.

Thank you to Lucinda Sharp, Director at Forty South Publishing. Thanks also to Kent Whitmore, designer, Rayne Allinson, Assistant Publisher, and to all the team at Forty South. A book doesn't happen without an enormous amount of input and support from others, and would not be on our bookshelves if publishers, such as Lucinda, didn't do what they do. Lucinda does it well.

Finally, I would like to give special thanks my son, Tom, a great supporter, always, and to my daughter, Kylie, who did the early design work for my novel. It is because of the both of you, and my parents, Irene and Graeme, that *Undertow* exists.

# About the author

Kim Bambrook is an author, poet, and adventurer. She has two adult children who motivate her daily.

Kim was a whimsical child prone to wandering the paddocks of her childhood farm in East Gippsland, Victoria. She entered adulthood seeking adventure and exploration. While travelling solo across the globe on foot, and by bicycle, Kim did not envision that her first novel – *Undertow* – would be inspired by adventures at sea.

Enticed by the ultimate sea change of living aboard a yacht, Kim moved to Tasmania twelve years ago. It was here that she learned to sail. Experiences in the Southern Ocean – unexpected, exhilarating and, on occasion, life threatening – gave Kim's pen new power.

Kim currently lives on the Freycinet Peninsula. She continues her exploration of wild places, writing book in hand.

kimbambrook.com